PROTECTING THE DESERT HEIR

BY
CAITLIN CREWS

Harlequin (UK) Limited's policy is to use papers that are
renewable and recyclable products and made from wood
sustainable forests. The logging and manufacturing proc-
to the legal environmental regulations of the country of o-

Printed and bound in Spain
by CPI, Barcelona

MILLS
&
BOON

Published in Great Britain 2015
by Mills & Boon, an imprint of Harlequin (UK) Limited,
Eton House, 18-24 Paradise Road, Richmond, Surrey, TW9 1SR

© 2015 Caitlin Crews

ISBN: 978-0-263-24877-7

USA TODAY bestseller and RITA® Award-nominated author **Caitlin Crews** loves writing romance. She teaches her favourite romance novels in creative writing classes at places like UCLA Extension's prestigious Writers' Programme, where she can finally utilise the MA and PhD in English Literature she received from the University of York in England. She currently lives in California, with her very own hero and too many pets. Visit her at caitlincrews.com

Visit the author profile page at millsandboon.co.uk for more titles

CHAPTER ONE

THE LAST TIME she'd run for her life, Sterling McRae had been a half-wild teenager with more guts than sense. Today it was more a *waddle* for her life than anything approaching a run—thanks to the baby she carried and had to protect no matter what, now that Omar was dead—but the principle remained the same.

Get out. Get away. Go somewhere you can never be found.

At least this time, twelve years older and lifetimes wiser than that fifteen-year-old who'd run away from her foster home in Cedar Rapids, Iowa, she didn't have to depend on the local Greyhound bus station to make her getaway. This time, she had limitless credit cards and a very nice SUV at her disposal, complete with a driver who would take her wherever she asked to go.

All of which she'd have to ditch once she got out of Manhattan, of course, but at least she'd start her second reinvention of herself with a little more style.

Thank you, Omar, Sterling thought then. The heels she refused to stop wearing even this late into her pregnancy clicked against the floor of the apartment building where she and Omar had shared his penthouse ever since they'd met while he'd been a graduate student. A wave of grief threatened to take her feet right out from under her, but Sterling fought it back with grim determination and clenched her teeth tightly as she kept on walking.

There was no time left for grief or anything else. She'd seen the morning news. Rihad al Bakri, Omar's fearsome older brother and now the ruler of the tiny little port country on the Persian Gulf that Omar had escaped at eighteen, had arrived in New York City.

Sterling had no doubt whatsoever that he would be coming for her.

There was every chance she was already being watched, she cautioned herself as she hurried from the elevator bank—that the sheikh had sent some kind of advance team to come for her even though the news had broadcast his arrival barely a half hour ago. That unpleasant if realistic thought forced her to slow down, despite the hammering of her heart, so she *appeared* nothing but calm. It forced her to smile as she moved through the lobby, the way she might have on any other day. There would be no honoring Omar if she let herself—and more important, her baby—fall into the clutches of the very people he'd worked so hard to escape. And she knew a little bit about the way predators reacted when they saw prey act like prey.

The more fearful you acted, the harder they attacked. Sterling knew that firsthand.

So instead, she walked. She *sauntered*.

Sterling walked like the model she'd been before she'd taken her position at Omar's side all those years ago. Like the notorious, effortlessly sensual mistress of the international playboy Omar had been in the eyes of the world. She strolled out into the New York

City morning and didn't look around to savor the great sprawl of the city she'd always loved so much and so fiercely. There was no time for goodbyes. Not if she wanted to keep her baby—Omar's baby—safe.

And she might have lost Omar, but God help her, she would not lose this baby, too.

Sterling was glad the summer morning was bright and warm, giving her an excuse to hide her thick grief and her buzzing anxiety and the too-hot tears she refused to let fall behind a pair of oversize sunglasses. It took her longer than it should have to realize that while that was indeed Omar's gleaming black SUV pulled up to the curb on the busy Upper East Side street, that was not Omar's regular driver standing beside it.

This man lounged against the side of the vehicle looking for all the world as if it was some kind of throne and he its rightful king. His attention was on the cell phone in his hand, and something about the way he scrolled down his screen struck Sterling as insolent. Or maybe it was the way he shifted and then looked up, his powerfully disapproving dark gaze slamming into hers with the force of a blow.

Sterling had to stop walking or fall over—and this time, grief had nothing to do with it.

Because that look felt like a touch, intimate and lush. And despite all the work Sterling had put into her image as a woman who wallowed neck-deep in the pleasures of the flesh, the truth was she did not like to be touched. Ever.

Not even like this, when she knew it wasn't real.

It *felt* real.

This driver was too much. Too tall, too solid. Too damned *real* himself. He was dressed in a dark suit,

which only served to make his lean, intensely dangerous body seem *lethal*. He had thick black hair, cut short
as if to hide its natural curl, rich brown skin and the
most sensual mouth Sterling had ever seen on a man
in her life, for all that it was set in a grim line. He was
astonishingly, noticeably, almost shockingly beautiful, something that should have been at odds with that
knife-edged form of his. Instead, it was as if he was a
steel-tempered blade with a stunningly bejeweled hilt.

He was either the last person she should want driv-
ing her to freedom, or the first, and Sterling didn't have
time to decide which. She didn't have any time at all.
She could feel her phone buzzing insistently from the
pocket where she'd stashed it, and she knew what that
meant.

Rihad al Bakri. The king himself, since his and
Omar's father had died a few years back. He was finally here, in Manhattan, as she'd feared. Both Omar's
friends and hers were texting her warnings, calling to
make sure she was aware of the impending threat. Because no matter what else happened, no matter what
might become of Sterling now without the man who
had been everything to her, Omar's older brother could
not know about this baby.

It was why she'd taken such pains to hide the fact that
she was pregnant all these months. Until today, when it
didn't matter any longer, because she was running away
from this life. She'd do what she'd done the last time.
A far-off city. Hair dye and/or a dramatically different
cut. A new name and a new wardrobe to go along with
it. It wasn't hard to pick a new life, she knew—it was
only hard to stick to it once you'd chosen it, because

ghosts were powerful and seductive, especially when you were lonely.

But she'd done it before, when she'd had much less. She had even more reason to do it now.

All of this meant that Sterling certainly didn't have time to ogle the damned driver, or wonder what it said about her that the first man she'd noticed in years seemed to have taken an instant dislike to her, if the strange driver's expression was any guide. It said nothing particularly good about her, she thought. Then again, maybe it was just her grief talking.

"Where is Muhammed?" she asked crisply, forcing herself to start forward again across the sidewalk.

The new driver only stared at her and as she drew closer she found herself feeling something like *sideswiped* by the bold, regal line of his nose and the fact that those dark eyes of his were far more arresting up close, where they gleamed a dark gold in the bright morning light. She was breathless and fluttery and she couldn't make any sense of it, nor understand why he should look something like *affronted*. Her phone kept vibrating, her breath was ragged and she was *this close* to bursting into tears right there on the street, so she ignored the odd beauty of this strangely quiet and watchful man and wrenched open the door to the SUV herself.

"I don't actually care where he is," she threw at him, answering her own question as her panic started to bang inside her like a drum. "Let's go. I'm sorry, but I'm in a terrible hurry."

He leaned there against the driver's window, his expression startled and thoughtful all at once, and he only studied her in a leisurely sort of way as Sterling slung her oversize shoulder bag inside. And she had never been much of a diva, no matter how much money Omar had given her to throw around. But today was a terrible day after a week of far worse, ever since she'd gotten that call in the middle of the night from the French police to tell her that Omar was dead after a terrible car crash outside Paris. And she had none of the social graces she'd worked so hard to learn left inside of her after that. Not even a polite word.

Not for a man like this one, who stared at her as if he would decide when and where they went, not her. Something snapped inside of her and she let it—hell, she welcomed it. A surly driver was a far better target than herself or Omar's terrifying brother, who, Sterling was well aware, could show up at any moment and destroy everything.

As far as she'd ever been able to tell from reading between the lines of Omar's staunchly loyal stories, that was pretty much all the sheikh did.

"How did you get this job?" she demanded, focusing her temper and her fear on the stranger before her. "Because I don't think you're any good at it. You do realize you're supposed to open the door for your passengers, don't you?"

"Yes, of course," he said then, and Sterling was so startled by that rich, low, deeply sardonic voice that she curled a hand around her big, low belly protectively even as her throat went alarmingly and suddenly dry. "My mistake. It is, of course, my single goal in life to serve American women such as yourself. My goal and my dream in one."

Sterling blinked. Had he said that in another way, she might have ignored it. But the way he *looked* at her.

As if he was powerful and hungry and *ferocious* and was only barely concealing those things beneath his civilized veneer. It arrowed into her, dark and stirring.

It reminded her, for the first time in a very long while, or maybe ever, that she was a woman. Not merely mother to her best friend's child, but entirely *female* from the top of her head, where that look of his made her feel prickly, all the way down to her toes, which were curling up in her shoes where she stood on the curb.

And entirely too many places in between.

The baby chose that moment to kick her, hard, and Sterling told herself *that* was why she couldn't breathe. *That* was why her entire body felt taut and achy and very much like someone else's.

"Then yours must be a life of intense disappointment," she told him when she could breathe again, or anyway, fake it. "As you fall so far short."

"My apologies," the driver replied at once, his voice smooth, but with that hard undercurrent in it that made Sterling's head feel light. "I forget myself, clearly."

He straightened then and that didn't make it any better. He was tall and broad at once, a sweep of black that took over the entire world, and she wouldn't have been at all surprised if he'd snatched her up, belly and all, in one powerful fist—

But he didn't. Of course he didn't. He reached over and wrapped his hand over the top of the door instead, then inclined his head toward the SUV's interior as if it was his car and he was the one doing her a great favor.

Impossible images chased through her head then, each more inappropriate and embarrassing and *naked* than the last. What was *wrong* with her? Sterling didn't

have thoughts like that, so yearning and wild. So...
unclothed. She didn't like to be touched at all, much
less...*that.*

"Well," she said stiffly after a tense, electric moment
she could feel everywhere, even if she couldn't understand it. She felt weak and singed straight through and
she couldn't seem to look away from him when she
knew that he was causing this. That it was *him.* "Try
not to do it again."

His dark gold eyes got more intense, somehow, and
that stunning mouth of his shifted into something that
could only be described as *mocking.* She ordered herself not to shiver in response, but she felt it wash over
her anyway, as if she had.

"But we really do have to get moving." She made her
voice softer then. Placating, the way she'd learned to
do with all kinds of men—all kinds of *people,* come to
think of it—over the years. She'd made it her art, and
no matter that her life with Omar had tempted her to
believe she wouldn't have to live like that any longer.
That she could turn it on or off for fun, as she wished.
There's no such thing as a happy ending, she reminded
herself harshly. *Not for you.* "I have a long way to go
and I'm already behind schedule."

"By all means, then," he said invitingly, the way a
wolf might have done, with the suggestion of claws and
the hint of fangs yet nothing but that sardonic smile on
his shockingly sensual, infinitely dangerous mouth.
"Get in. I would hate to inconvenience you in any way."

Then he reached out and took her hand, ostensibly
to help her into the SUV.

And it was like fireworks.

It was pure insanity.

Sensation galloped through her, shooting up from that shocking point of contact like wildfire, enveloping her. Changing her. Making the city disappear. Making her whole history fall out of her own head as if it had never happened. Making her body feel tight and restless and dangerously loose at once. Making her wonder, yearn, *long*—

She wanted to jerk her hand away from his, the way she always did when someone touched her without her permission, but she didn't. Because for the first time in as long as she could remember, Sterling wanted to *keep touching him* more than she wanted to stop.

That astounding truth pounded through her like adrenaline, a sleek and dizzying drum.

"I cannot serve you if you do not enter the vehicle," the driver said after a moment, his gaze narrowing in on hers in a way that made her breath go shallow. And his voice seemed to stoke the fires that raged in her, as if the way his hand wrapped around hers was a sexual act. A whole lot of sexual acts. "And that would be a tragedy, would it not?"

Sterling couldn't breathe. She couldn't *breathe*—and she was terribly afraid that the edgy feeling swamping her just then wasn't panic at all. She knew panic. This was deeper. Richer.

Life-altering, she thought in a kind of awe.

But the only thing she could let herself think about right now was her baby, so she shoved all the confusing sensations away as best she could—and tried to get into the car and get away from him before her legs simply gave out beneath her.

Or before she did something she'd truly regret, like moving closer to this strange man instead of away.

* * *

There were a number of things Rihad al Bakri—reigning sheikh, Grand Ruler and King of the Bakrian Empire—did not understand.

First, how his late brother had neglected to mention that he had impregnated his mistress and quite some time ago, if her current condition was any guide. Or how this one delicate American woman had managed to elude his entire security force and was now sashaying out into the city as if she was still on the sort of catwalks she'd frequented when she'd been, by all accounts, a feral teen. Finally, he was arrogant enough to wonder how on earth she could possibly have mistaken him—*him*—for a livery driver, of all things.

And that was not even getting into his unending grief that his brother was gone. That after wasting so many years of his life gallivanting about with this unsuitable woman, Omar could have disappeared so senselessly in the space of a single evening.

Rihad could not come to terms with it. He doubted he ever would.

Yet all of that faded when Rihad took her hand, meaning only to help her into the SUV as any decent servant might. He had enough of them. He should know.

The loud, brash, concrete city all around them seemed to skip its groove like an old-fashioned record, and go still.

So still it was like a quiet agony, reverberating inside of him.

Her hand was delicate and strong at once, and Rihad didn't like that. Nor did he like the way her mouth firmed as she looked at him, as if she was pressing her lips together to disguise the way they trembled, because he had the wild, nearly ungovernable desire to taste that theory.

Surely not.

Her strawberry blond hair should have appeared messy, twisted back in a riot of smooth gold and copper strands, but instead made her look fresh. She wore a stretchy sort of tunic dress over skinny jeans and absurdly high heels, quite as if she wasn't so heavily pregnant that it looked as if she'd shoved a giant ball underneath her clothes. Worst of all, she was remarkably graceful, moving easily from the sidewalk into the vehicle, making him wonder exactly how she might move when not pregnant.

Or better yet, beneath him.

Rihad did not want to wonder about this woman in any capacity at all and much less that one. He'd wanted nothing more than to eradicate the stain of her from the memory of his brother's life, erase her taint from the Bakrian royal family once and for all. That was why he'd come here himself, straight from Omar's funeral, when he could easily have sent agents to eject her from this property.

Enough scandal. Enough selfish, heedless behavior. Rihad had spent his life cleaning up his father's messes, Omar's messes, even his half sister Amaya's messes. Sterling McRae was the emblem of his family's licentiousness and Rihad wanted her—and all the remnants of his brother's lifetime of poor decisions—gone.

So naturally she was pregnant.

Hugely, incontestably, irrevocably pregnant.

Of course.

CHAPTER TWO

"YOU ARE WITH CHILD," Rihad said grimly as his brother's mistress settled herself in the SUV, pulling her hand from his as she sat—and perhaps, he thought, with a certain alacrity that suggested that simple touch had affected her, too.

He opted not to consider that too closely.

"You are very observant." Was that…sarcasm? Directed at *him*? Rihad blinked. But she continued, her voice now coolly imperious. "And now if you'll close the door and *drive*?"

She was giving him orders. She expected him—*him*—to obey these orders. To obey *her*.

That was such an astonishing development that Rihad merely stepped back and shut the door while he processed the situation. And thought about how to proceed.

All Rihad could hope for was that the child this woman carried was not Omar's—but he was not optimistic. His brother's obsession with his regrettable mistress had spanned the better part of a decade. Omar had famously scooped her up when she'd been a mere seventeen. He'd installed her in his apartment within the week, not caring in the least that she was little more than an ignorant guttersnipe with a made-up name who wasn't even of legal age at the time.

The paparazzi had all but turned gleeful cartwheels in the streets.

"Omar will tire of her," their late father had said after scanning one such breathless and insulting article, back in the Bakrian palace.

The old sheikh had been a connoisseur of flagrantly inappropriate women. He'd stopped marrying them after the mercenary Ukrainian dancer—the mother of the deeply disobedient Amaya, who was chief among Rihad's many problems these days while she evaded her responsibilities and the fiancé she'd decided she didn't want on the eve of her engagement party—had taken off and proceeded to live off the telling of her "my life in the evil sheikh's harem" story for decades. The old man had gone off matrimony after that, but not women. If anyone knew how men treated their mistresses, it would be his father.

"Perhaps a refresher course in your expectations of Omar might not go amiss," Rihad had suggested drily. "His time in New York City appears to have affected his memory, particularly where his duties to this country are concerned."

His father had only sighed, as Rihad had known he would. Because while Rihad was his father's heir, he had never been his father's favorite. And no wonder. Omar and the old sheikh were peas in a deeply selfish pod, stirring up scandals left and right as they did exactly as they pleased no matter the consequences, while Rihad was left to quietly clean it all up in their wake.

Because somebody had to be responsible, or the

country would fall to its enemies. That somebody had been Rihad for as long as he could remember.

"No man is without his weaknesses, Rihad," his father had said, frowning at him. "It is only regrettable that Omar is making his so public."

Rihad had no idea if he had weaknesses or not, as he'd never been given any leave to indulge them. He'd never kept mistresses, inappropriate or otherwise. He'd known full well that as his father's successor he'd been promised in a political marriage since birth. And he'd dutifully married the woman picked out for him when he'd finished his studies in England, in fulfillment of that promise.

Tasnim might not have been a flashy model type, with masses of shining copper-blond hair and a sinful mouth like the woman Omar had holed up with all these years. But she'd been as committed to their marriage as Rihad had been. They'd worked their way to something like affection in the three short years before she'd been diagnosed with cancer at a routine doctor's appointment. When she'd died five years ago this past summer, Rihad had lost a friend.

Maybe that was what moved in him then, on the side of a New York City street as his brother's worst and most public embarrassment sat waiting for him to drive her away from the comeuppance Rihad had planned to deliver upon her, in spades. Fury that Tasnim, who had kept all her promises, was gone. The same old mix of fury and bafflement that Omar had broken all the rules, as usual, and gotten this plaything of his big with child anyway—and then abandoned a Bakrian royal child to fate, its mother unmarried and unprotected.

That or the fact her hand in his, her skin sliding

against his in even so simple and impersonal a touch, had made him burn. He could feel it now. Still.

Unacceptable.

If he'd been anyone else, he thought, he might have been shaken by that astonishing burst of heat. Altered, somehow, by that fire that roared through him, making him feel bright and needy, and suggesting all manner of possibilities he didn't wish to face.

But Rihad was not anyone else. He did not acknowledge weakness. He rose above it.

He pulled out his mobile, made a call and snapped out his instructions as he climbed into the driver's seat, his decision made in an instant. Because it was the most expedient way to handle the crisis, he assured himself, not because he could *still* feel her touch as if she'd branded him. He could see Sterling in the back via his mirror—such a fanciful, ridiculous name—and the frown she aimed at him. It had nothing to do with the things that coursed through him at the sight of her, none of which he'd expected. He was a man of duty, never of need.

"You can't talk on your phone while you drive," she told him. *Scolded him*, more like. "You know that, don't you?"

As if he was extraordinarily dim. It occurred to Rihad then that no one he was not related to by blood, in all his years on this earth, had dared address him with anything but the utmost respect—if not fawning deference.

Ever.

For a moment he was stunned.

He should have been outraged. He couldn't understand why instead there was a part of him that wanted only to laugh.

"Can I not?" he asked mildly, after a moment, his tone an uneasy balance between the two. "I appreciate the warning."

"Aside from the fact it's against the law, it's not safe," she replied in that same irritated way he'd never in his life had directed at him before, her voice tight. *Annoyed*, even. He saw her shift against the leather seat and put her hands over her swollen belly, in a way that suggested she was not quite the soulless, avaricious harlot he'd painted her in his head. He ignored that suggestion.

"I don't think I'd care if you ran this car into the side of a building if it was only me, but it's not."

"Indeed it is not." Rihad slid his phone into the interior pocket of his jacket and then started the vehicle. "Yet your husband would miss you, surely?"

He was needling her, of course, and he couldn't have said why. What could he possibly gain from it? A glance in the rearview mirror showed him her profile, however, not that cool frown he found he very nearly enjoyed. She'd turned her head as if to stare back at the building as he pulled the car into traffic. As if leaving it—this place she'd lived with his brother, or *off* his brother if he was more precise—was difficult for her.

Rihad supposed it must have been. It would be much harder to find a patron now, no doubt. She was older, for one thing. Well-known—infamous, even—for her role as another man's prize possession, across whole years. Soon to be a mother to another man's child, which the sort of men who regularly trafficked in mistresses would be unlikely to find appealing.

Because you find her so unappealing even now, when

she is huge with your brother's child, a derisive voice inside chided him. *Liar.*

Rihad ignored that, too. He could not find himself attracted to his brother's infamous leftovers. He would not allow it.

"The father of my child is dead," Sterling said, her voice so frozen that if he hadn't stolen that glance at her, he'd have believed she really was utterly devoid of emotion.

"And you loved him so much you wish to follow him into that great night?" He couldn't quite keep the sardonic inflection from his own voice, and her head swung back toward him, her lovely brow creasing again. "That seems a rather desperate form of tribute, don't you think? The province of the cowed and the cowardly, in my opinion. Living is harder. That's the point of it."

"Am I having an auditory hallucination?"

That was obviously a rhetorical question. Still, Rihad shrugged as he turned onto the narrow highway that clung to the east side of the city and led out of town, and replied, "I cannot answer that for you."

"Or are you quizzing me—in a snide manner—about the death of someone I loved? You're a *driver.*"

And her tone was withering, but there was something about it that spoke of repressed emotions, hidden fears. Or perhaps he was the one hearing things then.

"I don't care what you think about my life or my choices or my feelings, in case that's not clear. I want you to drive the damned car upstate, no more and no less. Is that all right with you? Or do you have more unsolicited opinions to share?"

Rihad smiled as he merged onto a different highway and headed toward the top of the island and the stately bridge that would lead to the airfield where his jet should be waiting, refueled and ready, upon his arrival. Or heads would roll.

"Where are you going?" he asked her with deceptive casualness. "Upstate New York is lovely in the summer, but it is not possible to outrun anything in your condition. Surely you must realize this."

"My condition." She repeated the words as if, until she sounded them out, she couldn't believe she'd heard them correctly. "I beg your pardon?"

"You look as if you're used to being kept well," Rihad continued. Mildly. "That will be hard to replicate."

She swiped those huge, concealing sunglasses off her face, and Rihad wished she hadn't. She was nothing less than perfection, even in a quick glance in the rearview mirror of a moving vehicle, and he felt as if he'd been kicked by a horse. Her eyes were far bluer than the sky outside and she was more delicate, somehow, than she appeared in photographs. More vulnerable, he might have thought, had she not looked so outraged.

"Does it make you feel good to insult people you don't know?" she demanded, also in a tone he'd never heard directed at him before. This woman seemed to be full of such tones. "Is that the kind of man you are?"

"What kind of man I am or am not is hardly something you will be capable of ascertaining from the backseat of this vehicle."

"Yet you feel perfectly comfortable shredding my character from the front, of course. What a shock."

Rihad didn't like the tightness in his chest then. "Were you not kept well? Please accept my condolences. Perhaps you should have found a better patron before you permitted such a shoddy one to impregnate you."

He didn't know what he expected. Floods of tears? But Sterling sat straighter in her seat, managing to look both regal and dignified, which only made that constriction around his chest pull tighter.

"Let me guess," she said after a hard pause, her tone so scathing she was clearly nowhere near tears of any kind. "This is some kind of game to you. You intrude upon people's lives, insult them, and then what? Is causing pain its own reward—or are you hoping they'll do something crazy to get away from you, like demand you leave them by the side of the road? Exactly what do you get out of being this nasty?"

Rihad's teeth were on edge, his body tense. He left the bridge behind him and headed west, wanting absolutely nothing at that moment but to get to his plane and get the hell out of here, back to his own land. His throne. The familiarity of his country, his rule. Before the tension in him exploded into something he couldn't control.

That such a thing had never happened before—that he had never been quite this tense in the whole of his life before he'd laid eyes on this woman—did not bear thinking about.

"I have no intention of leaving you by the side of the road," he assured her, and there was possibly too much dark intent in the comment, because she scowled at him in response. "Not yet anyway."

"You're a true gentleman. Clearly."

And Rihad laughed then, because it was funny. All of this was funny, surely, however little familiarity he had with such things. He was a king pretending to be a driver. She was the mistress who had ruined his dead brother's life. And he felt more alive trading insults with her than he had in years.

In fact, he couldn't recall when he'd ever felt quite like this, for any reason.

He'd obviously gone mad with guilt and grief.

"I want us both to be very clear about who you are," Sterling said then, leaning forward in her seat, and her scent teased at him, honey and sugar with the faintest hint of a tropical bloom beneath. It made his hands clench into fists against the steering wheel. It made him hard and needy.

It made him feel like a stranger to himself. Like the hungry, selfish man he'd never been.

Rihad couldn't bring himself to analyze it. He concentrated on the road instead.

"I am perfectly clear about who I am," he told her.

Or perhaps he was telling himself—because he had been. When he'd exited his private jet mere hours before. When he'd arrived at Omar's apartment building, dismissed the driver who waited there and sent his team inside to secure this woman so he could have the pleasure of evicting her himself. He'd known exactly who he was.

And nothing has changed since then, he told himself harshly.

Or would.

"You are a man who thinks it's appropriate to mock and insult a woman, first of all," Sterling said in that precise way of hers that he really shouldn't find so fascinating. It was only that no one had ever dared use a tone like that in his presence before, he assured himself. He was intrigued intellectually, nothing more. "Congratulations. Your mother must be proud."

He laughed again, with significantly less mirth than before. "My mother died when I was twelve years old."

"A great blessing, I think we can agree, so that she might be spared the knowledge of who you've become in her absence," Sterling said, so matter-of-factly it took Rihad a moment to realize how deeply she'd insulted him. And then she kept going, unaware that no one spoke to him like that without consequences. No one would dare. "You are also a man who finds it amusing to speculate about the lives of strangers. Openly and repulsively."

"Are you not a kept woman?" he asked, making no attempt to soften his tone. "My mistake. What is it you do, then, to support yourself?"

"You are ill-mannered and rude, and that was evident at a glance, long before you opened your mouth." She laughed then, an abrasive sound that made his hackles rise. "I've met more honorable pigs."

"Be very careful," Rihad warned her. Because he had limits—even if, he was well aware, anyone who'd ever met him might have thought he'd crossed them a long while back. "A man does not react well to the questioning of his honor."

"Then a man should act as if he has some," she snapped.

"Yes, of course," Rihad snorted. "And how would I prove that I am an honorable man to one such as you, do you imagine? Will you be the judge? A woman who—"

"Is pregnant?" Her voice was icy then, so cold he almost overlooked the fact that she'd interrupted him. Something no one had done since his father had died, and no *woman* had ever done, as far as he could recall. "So scandalous, I know. It's almost as if every single person walking this earth came about their presence here some other way."

"I must have mistaken you for someone else," Rihad murmured as he made the final turn that would lead them to the airfield, which was just as well, because he thought his temper might flip the damned SUV over if he didn't put some distance between the two of them, and soon. "I thought you were the mistress of Omar al Bakri."

"If I were you—" and her voice was very soft, very furious then "—I'd be very, very careful what you say next."

"Why?" Rihad realized he was taking out his aggression on the gas pedal and slowed as he arrived at the gate to find his men already there, which was lucky for everyone involved. They waved him through and he was glad, he told himself, that this little farce was almost finished. He wasn't one for subterfuge, no matter how necessary. It felt too much like lies. "He is dead, as you say. You remain. Is that child his?"

"Ah, yes. Of course." She sounded bored then, though he could still hear the fury beneath it, giving it a certain huskiness that he felt in all the wrong places. "I must be a whore. That's the point of these questions, isn't it? Are you trying to determine whether or not I'm a terrible, no-good, very bad harlot or have you already rendered your judgment?"

"Are you?"

She laughed. "What if I am? What is it to you?"

But Rihad glanced at her in the mirror and saw the truth of things in the way her hands clasped on the shelf of her belly, her knuckles white, as if she was not as blasé as she was pretending.

It would be easier if she was. Easier, but it wouldn't

do much for that thing that still held him in its grip, that he refused to examine any closer.

"I'm only using the proper terminology to describe your role," he said mildly as he pulled up beside his plane out on the tarmac. "I apologize if you find that insulting."

"You decided I was a whore the moment you saw me," she said dismissively. Or he assumed that was what that particular tone meant, having never heard it before. "But virgins and whores are indistinguishable, I hate to tell you."

"It's a bit late to claim virginity, I think."

"Whores don't have identifying marks to set them apart." If she'd heard him, she was ignoring him— another new sensation for Rihad. He was beginning to feel each of them like blows. "Purity isn't a scent or a tattoo. Neither is promiscuity, which is lucky, or most men like you who love to cast stones would reek of it."

"I am aware of only one case of a virgin birth," he pointed out as he put the SUV into Park. "Everyone else, I am fairly certain, has gone about it the old-fashioned way. Unless you are on your way to notify the world's religious leaders of the second coming of Mary? That would explain your hurry."

"How many people have you slept with?" she asked, sounding unperturbed.

He laughed as much to cover his astonishment at her temerity as anything else. "Are you petitioning to be the next?"

"If you've slept with anyone at all and you're unmarried, you're a hypocrite."

"I am widowed."

A typical female might have apologized for his loss,

but this was Sterling McRae, and she was not, he was already far too aware in a variety of increasingly uncomfortable ways, the least bit *typical*.

"And you've never touched a single woman in your whole life save your late wife?"

He should not have brought Tasnim into this. He was furious with himself. And Sterling, of course, correctly interpreted his silence.

"Oh, dear," she murmured. "It appears you are, in fact, a hypocrite. Perhaps you should judge others a bit less. Or perhaps you're no more than one of those charming throwbacks who think chastity only matters when it's a woman's."

"The world has turned on its ear, clearly," Rihad said in a kind of wonder, as much to the tarmac as to her, and he told himself that what surged in him then was relief that this was over. This strange interlude as a man people addressed with such stunning disrespect. "I am being lectured to by a blonde American parasite who has lived off of weak and foolish men her entire adult life. Thank God we have arrived."

He turned in his seat, so he saw the way she jolted then, as if she hadn't noticed the SUV had come to a stop. She looked around in confusion, then those blue eyes of hers slammed back to his.

"What is this? Where are we?"

"This is an airport," Rihad told her, in that same patronizing, lecturing way she'd ordered him not to use his mobile as they'd driven out of Manhattan. "And that is a plane. My plane."

She went so white he thought she might topple over where she sat. Her hands moved over the round swell of her belly, as if she was trying to protect the child within from him, and he hated that there was some part of him that admired her for so futile a gesture.

"Who are you?" she whispered.

He suspected she knew. But he took immense satisfaction in angling closer, so he could see every faint tremor on those sinful lips. Every shiver that moved across her skin. Every dawning moment of horrified recognition in her deep blue gaze.

"I am Rihad al Bakri," he told her, and felt a harsh surge of victory as her gaze went dark. "If that is truly my brother's child you carry, it is my heir. And I'm afraid that means it—and you—are now my problem to solve."

CHAPTER THREE

THE SUV SEEMED to close in around her, her heart was a rapid throb in her throat and it was only another well-timed kick from the baby that broke through the panic. Sterling rubbed a hand over her belly and tried to calm herself.

He won't hurt you. He can't. *If this is the heir to his kingdom, you've never been safer in all your life.*

The man she should have realized wasn't the slightest bit subservient to anyone threw open the driver's door and climbed out of the SUV, then slammed it shut behind him. She could hear the sound of that voice of his outside on the tarmac, the spate of Arabic words like some kind of rough incantation, some terrible spell that he was casting over the whole of the private airfield. His men. *Her.*

And she couldn't seem to do anything but sit there, frozen in place, obeying him by default. She stared at the back of the seat he'd vacated and tried to convince herself that despite the panic stampeding through her veins, she really was safe.

She had to be safe, because this baby had to be safe.

But the truth was, there was more than a small part of her that was still holding out hope that this was all a terrible nightmare from which she'd bolt awake at any minute. That Omar would be there, alive and well, with that wry smile of his at the ready and exactly the right words to tease away any lingering darkness. He'd tell her none of this could possibly have happened. That it never would.

And this would be a convoluted, nonsensical story she'd tell him over a long, lazy breakfast out on their wraparound terrace with views of New York City stretching in all directions as if it really was the center of the world, until they both laughed so hard they made themselves nearly sick.

God, what she would do to wake up and find out this was all a bad dream, that Omar had never gotten in that car in France, that it had never spun out of control on its way back into Paris—

But the door beside her opened abruptly then and Rihad stood there before her.

Because, of course, it was him. Rihad. The sheikh. *The king.* The more-feared-than-respected ruler of his fiercely contested little country on the Persian Gulf. The older brother who had consistently made Omar feel as if he was a failure, despite how much Omar had looked up to him. As if he was less than Rihad somehow. As if the deepest truths of who he'd been had to be hidden away, lied about, concealed where no one could see them—especially not the brother who should have loved him unconditionally.

Omar had loved him, despite everything. Sterling had not been similarly handicapped.

"There has been no mention of this pregnancy in any of the papers," Rihad said in his dark, authoritative way. "No hint."

"Guess why?" she suggested, hoping all the pain she'd like to inflict on him was evident in her voice. "Guess who we didn't want to know?"

"You were both fools."

Sterling glared at Rihad as the light wrapped around him and made him look something like celestial. How had she managed to convince herself this man was merely a *driver*? He fairly *oozed* power from every pore. He was the physical embodiment of ruthlessness no matter how the summer sunlight loved him and licked over the planes and valleys of his fascinating face. He exuded ruthless masculinity and total authority in equal measure, and she'd thrown herself directly into his hands.

He stared down at her, that mouth of his in a sardonic curl, his dark gold gaze bright and hot and infinitely disturbing, until Sterling thought she might not be able to breathe normally again. Ever.

"I believe this is the part where a good driver helps a fine, upstanding lady such as yourself from the vehicle," he said in that smooth way of his, like silk and yet with all that steely harshness beneath it. "Without any commentary involving terms she might or might not like."

"I think you mean insults, not terms."

"I think it's time to get out of the car."

Then he held out his hand and there was no pretending it was anything but a royal command.

"I'm not getting on that plane," Sterling told him.

Very carefully and precisely, as if perfect diction might save her here. Save her from him. As if anything could.

"It was not a request."

She could see then how much he'd been *acting* the

part of the supposed servant before, because he wasn't bothering with that any longer. He was a stern column of inimitable power, his will like a living thing coiled tight around both of them and the whole damned airfield besides, and she couldn't understand why he'd played that game with her in the first place. This was not a man who pretended anything, ever, she understood at a glance. Because he didn't need to pretend. This was a man who took what he wanted as he wanted it, the end.

But she was not going to let him take her. Not without a fight.

"Perhaps you're misunderstanding me, Rihad," she said, deliberately using his first name to underscore how little she respected him.

She felt the ripple of that impertinence move through him and then beyond him, through the line of his men, where they stood in a loose ring around him and the SUV, protection and defense. The disapproval washed back over her from all sides, but the gleam in Rihad's dark gold gaze merely edged over into something more shrewd as he considered her.

As if she was an animal in a trap, she thought, and he was deciding how best to put her out of her misery. That was not a restful notion.

Sterling pushed on. "I would rather die than go anywhere with you."

He leaned toward her in the open wedge between the door and the body of the SUV and every single nerve inside of her went wild. Sharp and hot and *alert*—something so much like pain it very nearly toppled her before she realized it wasn't really pain at all. Merely an exquisite reaction—pure sensation, storming all over her—that she didn't recognize and didn't know what to do with.

It was almost impossible to keep herself from reacting, from throwing herself backward across the wide backseat and scrambling for safety—not that there was any available to her, she understood in a shattering instant. Not really. This man might not hurt her, physically, not as long as she was pregnant with the heir to his kingdom—but then, there were worse things.

She'd seen so many of them firsthand.

"Please believe me," Rihad said softly then, so softly, though, that it only made her understand on a deep, visceral level how truly lethal he was. "I would arrange that if I could."

"How charming," she breathed, trying desperately not to sound as panicked as she felt. "I love threats."

He smiled. "I would have done so years ago if I'd believed for one second that it would ever come to this. But let me assure you, any interest I appear to have in you is about the child you carry, not you. Never you."

"This is Omar's child," she snapped back at him, struggling to keep her jangling, shimmering reaction to him to herself. "And since he is gone, that makes the baby my responsibility, not yours."

"That is where you are wrong," Rihad told her, his tone as merciless as that harsh look on his forbidding face. "If that child is indeed my brother's—"

"Of course it is!" Sterling threw at him.

And only realized once she had said it that it was hardly strategic to tell him so. If he thought the child was someone else's, if she could have convinced him of that, he might have let her go. Something in that dangerous dark gold gleam in his gaze told her he'd reached the same conclusion.

"Then, as I have explained, it is potentially next in line to rule my country." He shrugged. "Your wishes would be of less than no importance to me at any time, but in a situation such as this? Which affects the whole of my country and its future?"

He didn't have to finish the thought. That hard, sardonic twist to his lush mouth did it for him.

She tried again. She had no choice. "I refuse to go anywhere with you."

"Get out of the car, Sterling," he ordered her, steel and warning, and there was nothing but sheer power in his gaze. It rolled through her like fire. Or perhaps that was her name in his mouth while he looked at her like that. "Or I will take you out of it myself. And I rather doubt you will enjoy that."

"Wow." Sterling let out a small, brittle laugh. "This has been quite a morning for exploring the dimensions of your character, hasn't it?"

"Hear this now," he replied, his voice a hoarse kind of softness that made her shiver, his gaze dark and so powerful as it held fast to hers. "There is nothing I wouldn't do for my country. Nothing at all."

"How heroic." But she was far more shaken by that than she should have been, when it wasn't even any kind of direct threat. "I think we both know the truth is less noble. You're nothing but a reactionary Neanderthal who is never challenged, never questioned, never forced to face the consequences of his actions."

"You appear to have your al Bakri brothers confused," Rihad replied with a certain soft menace that made her think she'd landed a blow. "I am not the renowned playboy who lived a life of leisure and debauchery. That was Omar. I am the one who cleaned up his messes. Again and again and again."

She wanted to scream. Throw things. But she only curled her hands into fists and glared. "I take it you mean me. I am the mess."

"You are not a mess, Sterling." He sounded kind, but she could see that look in his gaze, and she knew better. "You are a toxic spill. You corrupt and you destroy, and you have been doing it for over a decade. What you did to my brother was bad enough. It appalls me to think you will have your claws sunk deep in the next generation of al Bakris." His perfect lips firmed. "But I am a man of duty, not desire. Which means as much as I would prefer to pretend you and whatever child you carry do not exist, I cannot."

She couldn't breathe for a moment. It was almost too much. It threw her back in time to that terrible house in Iowa and the foster parents who had believed that she was nothing but their personal punching bag. Worthless and dirtied, somehow, by her own tragic history. And their contempt. For a moment she almost tipped back over into all that darkness—but then she caught his gaze again, so bright and hard at once, and it bolstered her. It lifted her.

Because she'd survived far worse than this man and *like hell* would she slide back into that headspace after a few mean words.

"Oh, no," she murmured icily. "You might get this toxic spill all over your sheikhdom. What then?"

"You'll find I am not so easily led astray," he said, his voice as low as hers had been, but layered with a kind of dark heat she could feel within her. Making her too warm in all kinds of places she didn't understand. "And I've had a lifetime of preparation. You're merely one more disaster it falls to me to handle."

"And then, oddly, you wonder why I don't want to go anywhere with you." She squared her shoulders. "I'm not afraid of you, Rihad."

And the strange thing was, she wasn't. He made her anxious, yes—panicky about the future. But that wasn't the same thing as *afraid*. She didn't know what to make of that. It didn't make any sense.

"Go ahead," Rihad suggested, those disturbingly bright eyes of his tearing into her, seeing far too much. "Fight me if you like. Scream loud enough to draw down the sun. Kick and scratch and hurl invective as it pleases you." He shrugged almost lazily, and Sterling's throat felt tight, while far to the south, parts of her she'd always largely ignored bloomed with a mad heat. "But this will still end the same way, no matter what you do. What is Omar's belongs to Bakri. And what is Bakri's is mine. And I will do what I must to protect what is mine, Sterling, even if it means I must kidnap you to accomplish it."

He straightened then, though his gaze never shifted from hers, and Sterling couldn't tell if that lump in her throat was panic or tears or something a good deal more like *fate*.

Don't be absurd, she snapped at herself, but that sensation of foreboding snaked down her back all the same.

"But by all means," he said, daring her in that soft way that danced along her limbs and made her skin prickle with warning, and something much warmer, "try me."

Sterling opted to decline that offer with as much icy

silence as she could muster. She also ignored his offered hand, but she pushed herself out of the SUV and
onto the tarmac anyway, because she'd always been a
realist at heart. Oh, her years with Omar had tempted
her to surrender to optimism, but deep down she'd always known better. She'd always known what lurked
down there beneath the happiest-seeming moments.
She'd always assumed, on some level, that it would all
end badly.

So she stood on her own two feet in front of this terrible man and she made the command decision to keep
playing her role. Sterling McRae, rich man's whore.
Toxic spill, no less. Coveted by many, captured by none
save Omar. She'd gotten very good at it. She reached up
and unclipped her strawberry blond hair, shaking her
head to send it tumbling down around her shoulders.
She shifted position so that her breasts were thrust out
and saw the very male response in his eyes.

All men were the same after all, even when a woman
was as far along as she was. Even kings.

"How long will you be kidnapping me for?" she
asked, so very politely.

"Ah, Sterling," he replied in the same tone, though
his look was far darker, and she had to fight back a be-
traying sort of flush when he shifted, the lean power of
his body too obvious, too *close*. "Haven't you guessed
yet how this must end?"

She eyed him with sheer dislike. "You dropping dead
where you stand, if there is a God."

He shook his head at her. "You can always take to
prayer, if you feel it will help. It won't change what must
happen, but perhaps you'll approach it all with some
measure of serenity."

"Is that what you call this? 'Serenity'?"

His fine, dark brows lifted. "I call it duty. I doubt you'd recognize it if you tripped over it."

"Says the man who already married a stranger on command once and thought that made him virtuous," she snapped, the past he'd thrown in Omar's face so often coming back to her then in a burst. "I'm more afraid of tripping over your ego than your duty."

"You don't know anything about my first marriage," Rihad told her with a lethal, vicious edge in his voice. "Not one single thing."

"I know that expecting Omar to make the same sacrifice was hideous," she said crisply, as if she wasn't the least bit shaken. Though still…not afraid of him, somehow. "And you can tell yourself any stories you want about me and my past and whatever else, but I had nothing to do with it. *I* was the only thing in his life he liked."

"Sterling."

His face was closed down then, granite and bone. Utterly forbidding.

"If this is where you bore me with self-serving lies about your idyllic arranged first marriage, I think I'll pass." She eyed him. "I'm not as big a fan of stories as you seem to be."

"It is my second marriage that should concern you, not my first."

She stared back at him. Then she understood, in a terrible rush that felt like a tide coming in, crashing over her and rolling her into the undertow, then sweeping her far out to sea. All in that instant.

"Do I know the lucky bride?" Sterling asked, her

voice as sharp as the razor-edged smile she aimed at him. "I'd like to convey my condolences."

"An heir to my kingdom cannot be born out of wedlock," he said, and she couldn't tell if that note in his voice was fury or satisfaction. Perhaps it was both. It thudded in her all the same. "You must realize this."

She jerked up her chin, belligerently. "I'm not marrying you. I'm not getting on that plane, I'm not letting you near my baby, and I'm definitely not *marrying* you. Your heirs are your own damned problem."

And the sheikh only smiled.

"I didn't ask you to marry me," he said softly. "I told you what was going to happen. Resign yourself to it or do not, it won't make any difference. It will happen all the same."

"You can't *tell* me to do anything," Sterling fired back at him, and she couldn't control the way she trembled then, as if he'd already clapped her in chains and carted her away to his far-off dungeon. "And you certainly can't make me *marry* you!"

"Pay attention, Sterling." Rihad's gaze was hotter than the summer sun, and far more destructive. And his will was an iron thing, as if he didn't require chains. She could feel it wrapped around her already, pressing against her skin like metal. "I am the King of Bakri. I don't require your consent. I can do whatever the hell I want, whenever I want. And I will."

CHAPTER FOUR

STERLING MARRIED SHEIKH RIHAD AL BAKRI, King of Bakri, at his royal palace on a lovely terrace overlooking the gleaming Bakrian Sea a mere two weeks later, surrounded by his assorted loyal subjects and entirely against her will.

Not that anyone appeared to care if the bride was willing. Least of all the groom.

"I don't want to marry this man," she told the assembled throng when Rihad walked her through the crowd as the ceremony began. "He is *forcing me* to marry him!"

She didn't expect that anyone would spring into action on her behalf, exactly, but she'd expected... something. Some kind of reaction. Some acknowledgment, however small, of what was happening to her. Instead, the collection of Bakrian aristocrats only gazed back at her. Indifferently.

"They don't speak English," Rihad murmured lazily from beside her, resplendent in his traditional robes in a way Sterling couldn't let herself look at too closely. It made her feel faint. Weak. Or maybe that was the way he held her arm as they walked, too strong and somehow too appealing there beside her, despite everything.

She didn't want to marry him. But she didn't seem to mind him touching her, and that contradiction was making her feel even crazier. "And even if they did, who do you think they would support? Their beloved king or the woman who led my brother down the path of wickedness?"

"Don't they have a problem with the fact you're marrying a woman who's carrying another man's child?"

But no one seemed particularly moved by that, either, when she knew they could hear her. *See* her. Least of all Rihad.

"They think I am a great hero, to protect the family honor in this way." He sounded so at his ease. It made the knot in her belly pulse in response. She told herself that was *dismay*. "To do my duty, a concept I know escapes you, despite the fact it requires I lower myself to marry a known harlot of no pedigree, less education and inadequate means."

He'd reduced her entire life into three cruel phrases. And not as if he was trying to slap at her as he did it, but as if he was merely stating the unsavory, unfortunate facts. Sterling's throat was impossibly dry. She was sure she was shaking. But he still held her arm in his easy grip, giving her the impression she could wrench herself away from him if she wanted. She knew better, somehow, than to test that.

"There's nothing preventing me from throwing myself over the side of that railing over there to escape you and save you from this great act of charity you're performing," she told him then, sounding far away even to her own ears. "What makes you think I won't?"

They stopped walking and stood before the small, wizened man she understood would marry them here, with the sea spread out before them like the promise of eternity—but it felt as much like a prison as the plane that had brought her here days ago had, or the rooms they'd stashed her in since, no matter how well-appointed. Inside of her, something ached. And she felt more than saw that infuriating, indolent shrug of his from where he stood next to her.

"Jump," Rihad invited her, low and dark. It shouldn't have moved in her the way it did, like fire and need, when he was only goading her. "It's a fifty-foot drop to the rocks below and, in truth, the answer to a thousand prayers for deliverance from you and all you represent." A small smile played over his mouth when she glared back at him. "Did you imagine I would beg you to reconsider? I am only so good, Sterling."

He was so certain she wouldn't do it. She could see it as if it was written across his darkly handsome face in block letters—and he was right. She'd survived too much, come too far, to take herself out now, even if there hadn't been a baby to consider.

It wasn't the first time she'd had to grit her teeth to make it through an unpleasant situation, she reminded herself staunchly. With a quick glance at the man taking up too much space beside her, implacable and fierce, Sterling rather doubted it would be the last.

Rihad hadn't hit her. He didn't seem violent at all, in fact, merely unimpressed with her. That was a long way from the worst place she'd ever been. She didn't want this—but it wouldn't kill her, either. So she trained her eyes on the officiant before them and surrendered.

And when there were no further disruptions from her, the wedding went ahead. Sterling felt it all from a great distance, as if she was watching a movie of that enormously pregnant woman in the billowing dress stand next to that darkly beautiful man with the smug expression on his face that indicated he'd had no doubt at all that she would do exactly as he pleased. Exactly what he wanted, as, apparently, everyone did eventually. It didn't seem to matter that she didn't participate in her own wedding ceremony, didn't speak a single word either way. No one asked her to do anything but stand there. The man marrying them merely waved his hands in her direction, Rihad answered him in impenetrable Arabic and that was that.

The crowd cheered when it was done, as if this was a happy occasion. Or, she supposed, as if it was a real wedding.

"I hate you," she told him, and bared her teeth at him. She didn't pretend it was any kind of smile. They stood there in all that distractingly cheerful sunshine, as if there really was some call for celebration in the midst of this disaster. When instead she was married to a man she loathed, trapped here in his world, his palace, his very hands. She told herself that was fury she felt, that low, shivering thing inside her, or the fact she couldn't seem to take in a full breath. Because she refused to let it be anything else. "I will always hate you."

"Always is a very long time, Sterling." Rihad sounded darkly amused. "I find most people lack the attention span for sustained emotion of any kind. Hate, love." He shrugged. "Passion is always brightest when temporary."

"You are an expert, of course."

"My expertise fades next to yours, of course, and all your fabled conquests," he replied, his tone ripe with bland insult.

"You have yet to marry a woman who actually *wants* to marry you," Sterling couldn't keep herself from railing at him, almost as if his insults got to her. Which she refused to allow. "I doubt you have the slightest idea what passion is."

Rihad's smile edged into something lethal, and while he didn't hurt her in any way when he took her arm, she couldn't pull out of his firm grasp, either. His smile deepened when she tried.

"You forget that I did not exactly choose you, either," he said, darkly and too hot and directly into her ear, making her shudder in reaction—and she was all too aware he could feel her do it. That made it worse, like some kind of betrayal. "I executed my duty to this country the first time I was married. Can you truly imagine I wanted to do it again?"

"Then you should have left me in New York."

"No." His voice was firm. Matter-of-fact. She saw the harsh intent in his golden gaze, stamped deep into the lines of his dark, gorgeous face. "That child cannot be born out of wedlock and also be recognized as a part of the royal bloodline. It isn't done."

"Omar said it would be fine," Sterling threw back at him as Rihad's aides corralled the well-heeled courtiers and herded them from their seats, directing them farther down the terrace. "He said it was the only child he planned to present to you and if you wanted it, or him, you could change the law. After all, you're the king."

"Of course," Rihad growled.

A muscle worked in his lean jaw and she felt his fingers press the slightest bit harder into the flesh of her upper arm where he still held her fast, though, still, it didn't hurt. Quite the opposite—she was astonished at the fact her usual revulsion at the faintest physical contact hadn't kicked in yet. It was her hatred of him, she told herself resolutely. It was shorting out her usual reactions.

"How typical of my brother," Rihad was saying. "Rather than adhere to a tradition dating back centuries, why not demand that the tradition itself be altered to suit him instead? I don't know why I'm at all surprised."

Sterling opened her mouth to argue, to defend Omar, but the dark look Rihad threw at her stopped her. She shut her mouth with an audible snap. And then he began to move, sweeping her along with him whether she wanted to go or not.

He led her back through the glorious royal palace to the suite of rooms she'd been installed in when she'd arrived, and Sterling was glad he did it in that fulminating, edgy silence of his. She felt utterly off balance. Shaken down deep. She couldn't tell if it was because the wedding had actually happened precisely as he'd warned her it would. Or because he kept *touching* her in a thousand little impersonal ways that were nonetheless like licks of fire all over her body and none of it because of fear.

Or because when he leaned down and spoke so close to her ear she'd felt it everywhere. *Everywhere.* Like the most intimate of caresses.

She still felt it. And she hadn't the slightest notion what to do about it.

It wasn't until they reached her door that Sterling realized she had no idea what was going to happen next. That she'd resolutely refused to believe this was happening at all, this mockery of a wedding, and had thus not thought about…the rest of it.

Did he expect...? Would he...? Her mind shied away from it, even as her body burst into a humiliating flash of delirious heat that she was terrified he could *see*, it felt so bright and scarlet and obvious. She clutched at her belly, as much to remind herself that she was hugely pregnant as to assuage her sudden spike in anxiety.

But Rihad merely deposited her inside the lovely, spacious suite that was the prettiest prison cell she'd ever seen, then turned as if to leave her there without another word—standing in the middle of the suite's grand foyer in an indisputably gorgeous dress her attendants had insisted she wear today, that had made Sterling feel pretty despite herself. Despite *him*.

"That's it?" she blurted out.

She wished she hadn't said anything when he turned back to her. Slowly. He was particularly beautiful then, in his ceremonial robes with that remote, inscrutable expression on his lean face. Beautiful and terrible, and she had no idea what to make of either.

But she didn't think it was fear that made her pulse pick up.

"What were you expecting?" he asked, mildly enough, though there was a dark gleam in those gold eyes of his that made her breath catch. "A formal wedding reception, perhaps, so you could insult my guests and my people with your surly Western attitude? Berate our culture and our traditions as you are so fond of doing? Shame this family—and me—even more than you already have?"

"You're not going to make me feel guilty about a situation all your own doing," she told him, ignoring the hint of shame that flared inside of her anyway, as if he had a point.

He does not have a point. He hurt Omar, kidnapped

you—but she could still feel it inside of her. As if her own body took his side over her own.

"Or perhaps you thought we should address the subject of marital rights. Did you imagine I would insist?" Rihad moved closer and Sterling held her breath, but he only stopped there a breath away from her, his gaze burnished gold on hers, and still too much like a caress. "I hate to disappoint you. But I have far better things to do than force myself on my brother's—"

Sterling couldn't hear him call her a whore on the day she'd married him. He'd come close enough out on the terrace. She couldn't hear him say it explicitly, and she didn't want to consider why that was. What that could mean.

"Don't let me keep you, then," she said quickly before he could say it. "I'll be right here. Hating you. Married to you. Trapped with you. Doesn't that sound pleasant?"

"That sounds like normal life led by married couples the world over," he retorted, and then he laughed. It seemed to roll through her and a smart woman, Sterling knew, would have backed away from him then. Found safer ground no matter if it looked like retreat. But she, of course, stood tall. "And yet there is nothing *normal* about this, is there?"

And something shifted then. The air. The light that danced in from outside her windows. Or, far more disturbing, that shimmering, electric thing that she worked so hard to pretend she couldn't feel there between them. It pulled taut. It gleamed there in his fascinating gaze, dark gold and intoxicating.

Maybe that was why she did nothing when he reached out and slid his hand over her jaw to cup her cheek. Nothing but let him, when she'd never *let* anyone touch her before. She only held that gaze of his and possibly her breath, too, as his hard dark gold eyes bored into her and the heat of his hand *changed* her, from the inside out, telling her things she'd never wanted to know about herself, because she felt so many things, so many wild and intense sensations, and none of them were *revulsion*—

"Damn you," he muttered, as if he was the cursed one. As if he was as lost as she was, as utterly out of control. "Everything about you is wrong."

Then he bent his head and fit his mouth to hers, claiming her as easily as if he'd done so a thousand times before. As if she'd been his forever.

And everything stopped. Then melted.

Sterling braced herself for the kick of panic, of horror, but it never came. There was only the heat of it, the banked fury, the rolling wildfire that swept through her and altered everything it touched.

It was long and hot, slow and thorough.

Astonishingly carnal. Deliriously perfect.

It was nothing like the kisses she'd imagined, locked safely away in her little world, where she was never at risk of having one. Rihad's kiss was possessive and devastating at once, storming through her, making her forget everything but him. Everything but this.

She forgot that she was anything but a woman—*his* woman, however he would have her, whatever it took, to burn in this fire until she was nothing but ash and longing, fire and need.

And his. God help her, she wanted to be *his*—

Rihad pulled away then and she could feel his breath against hers, harsh and stirring. Uneven, just as hers was.

He dropped his hand from the side of her face and stepped back, and it was as if he'd thrown them both out of vivid color and bright hot light into a cool, gray chill in that same instant. They only stared at each other for what felt like an eternity.

Sterling was aware of everything and nothing at once. The fine tapestries on her walls, in pinks and reds and ancient golds. The gilt and marble statuettes that bristled on every surface and the sparkling crystal that adorned the high chandeliers, every inch of which she'd studied in the long days she'd been here. The endless blue sea outside, putting the world right there in front of her yet always out of reach, so high up on the cliff side was the Bakrian royal palace. The baby inside of her, low and painful today, as if even her unborn child was expressing its disgust at what she'd let happen to her.

And Rihad. The king. Her husband. The man who had just *kissed* her. He looked every inch the wealthy sheikh today, in his traditional garments that only emphasized his strength, his power. The sheer intensity he carried with him like a sword, and now she knew he could wield it, too.

His expression was like stone as he gazed back at her, though his dark gold eyes burned the way she still did with the aftereffects of that kiss stampeding all over her, and Sterling couldn't bring herself to look away.

"Whatever you're about to say, don't." Her voice hardly sounded like hers, and she understood that it was far too revealing. That it told him far too much, and in far more depth. But she couldn't seem to help herself. "Not today."

Rihad's nostrils flared as if he was pulling in a deep,

deep breath, or fighting for control. As if he was as thrown by this as she was. As if the addictive taste of that wildfire that still crackled through her was too sharp, too dangerous, in him, too.

"I'm touched," he said, and she understood that was all wishful thinking on her part, thinking this was difficult for him. Nothing was, after all. Not for the king. "I had no idea our wedding meant so much to you, considering how bitterly you complained throughout it."

His voice was rough and sardonic, but Sterling was sick, she understood then, because she still felt the kiss like a caress. Her oversensitive breasts ached as if it had been that faintly calloused palm of his all over her bare skin. A little flicker of sensation skated from the tight peaks of each of them down through the center of her body to pool deep in her core. Then pulsed.

She'd always had a vivid imagination. But now what stormed in her was *need*.

"You don't know anything about me," she said, with what she thought was admirable calm, given the fact she now knew what that hard mouth of his felt like against hers, so hot and so male she might never recover from it.

"The trouble is, I know entirely too much about you," he said after a moment, his tone harsh and cool, while his golden gaze seemed to tear into her. "And despite the temptation, I can't overlook the fact that you were my brother's low-class tramp of a mistress for over a decade."

"And I am now also your wife," she pointed out, amazed that her voice sounded so much calmer than she felt, if not quite as regally cool as his. She tipped up her chin. "Congratulations on your choices."

"Let me be clear about how this marriage will work," he said, and something curled up inside of her at the way he said it. "You will stay here in the palace until you deliver the baby. Will you wish to nurse it?"

"I…" She felt as if he'd tossed her over the side of that terrace after all. One moment he was kissing her, all carnal longing and impossible heat, and the next he was interrogating her about her plans for the baby's feedings?

"I don't care if you do or do not," he said when she only blinked at him. "But if you do, you will stay here until the child is weaned. You will receive all the care and help you could require, of course. For all intents and purposes, that is now my child."

"Never," she said at once. Softly enough, but with feeling. "This is Omar's baby. *My* baby. Nothing you do can change that."

"Yes." And his voice was ferocious. "Omar's baby. Omar's mistress. Omar's many problems. This is nothing new for me, Sterling. I have been cleaning up after my brother all my life—why should it change now that he is dead?"

It was all too easy to remember how much she hated him then, and she clenched her hands so tightly into fists that her nails dug into her palms.

"What happens after the child is weaned?" she asked in a clipped voice as a tsunami of self-loathing crept ever closer, reminding her that she'd not only let this callous man touch her, but she'd also *liked* it. More than liked it.

She'd wanted more. Maybe she really was the whore

Rihad thought she was. Maybe the fact she'd never touched anyone had concealed the essential truth about her.

"That is entirely up to you," he said curtly. "Behave, and I may let you stay here, as long as you do not make a nuisance of yourself. Misbehave, and I will have you locked up in a remote part of the kingdom, a prisoner in fact and deed. I don't care which it is."

"I don't want this," she blurted out, because she was suddenly light-headed, and the thought that this was really her life now, that this had really happened, made the world spin.

He lifted a shoulder, then dropped it in that way of his—the royal sheikh untouched by and uninterested in such lowly concerns.

"Life is filled with sacrifices, Sterling." His voice scraped over her, so harsh she expected it had left marks. "There were always going to be consequences for your relationship with my brother, whether he told you so or not. This is but one of them."

She shook her head, as much to clear it as to negate him. "I don't understand why you won't let me go."

He considered her for a moment, and there was no reason at all Sterling should flush while he did.

"You cannot imagine I would release a member of my blood into your tender care, can you?" He sounded amazed. And that was so insulting it would have hurt, had not everything else hurt that much more already. "The child stays here. And if you have a shred of maternal feeling in you, which I doubt, so will you. A child needs its mother, I am reliably informed. Even if that mother is you."

"Wonderful," she managed to say then, her voice bitter and thick. "That sounds like quite a life sentence. How lucky I am to have been snatched off the street and forced into such an advantageous marriage with the most benevolent and thoughtful dictator around."

"If you weren't so appallingly self-centered, you'd see that you truly are lucky," he retorted, a flash of something dark in those eyes of his. "Far luckier than you deserve. But then, thinking of others is hardly your strong suit, is it? Or you'd have left my brother alone years ago."

"And a happy wedding day to you, too, Rihad," she threw back at him, and it was easier to simply hate him. Cleaner. Less complicated. It felt like a relief, and she didn't question why she felt so free to do it. "You're a terrible man and will no doubt be a worse husband, in much the same way I'm sure you're an awful king. Oh, joy."

Temper cracked over his face then, dark and alarming, and she braced herself for whatever awful thing he might say next—*whore whore whore, wash and repeat, whore whore whore,* she thought with a mental roll of her eyes that suggested an insouciance she didn't quite feel—but instead, he went still. Then frowned.

Not at her, exactly. More at the floor beneath her.

Sterling looked down to find a puddle around her, soaking the hem of her wedding dress and then spreading out across the inlaid mosaic tiles at her feet, and froze in horror. Had she actually humiliated herself to such a degree that she'd—

But then she understood.

The puddle announced what she should have guessed from her mounting discomfort throughout this conversation, but had been too furious and too emotional to face—that her water had broken.

Her baby was coming a few weeks early, whether she was ready or not.

CHAPTER FIVE

SOME THIRTY-SIX HOURS after he'd kissed the new wife he hadn't wanted in an act of dark foolishness that had haunted him ever since, Rihad stood in the shadows of Sterling's state-of-the-art hospital suite in the center of Bakri City and watched her sleep at last.

He didn't know why he was there, lurking about like a spurned lover instead of the king, when they had both been forced into this marriage, him by circumstance and her by his own hand. Instead, he couldn't seem to look away from Sterling, the woman he'd called a toxic spill.

He should not regret that. It was the truth, he knew, at least in terms of his brother's life this past decade. But it was hard to remember that at the moment.

There were the faintest smudges beneath her impossibly long lashes, the only indication he could see on her lovely face of how she'd spent the past day and a half. And she was so beautiful, so very nearly angelic in repose, that it made him realize he'd never seen her like this before—so vulnerable, so soft. Not fighting him, poking at him, insulting him or challenging him. Not plastered across tabloid magazines with her breasts falling out of her neckline and Omar's arm wrapped tightly around her.

Not toxic by any measure.

His chest felt too tight for his own ribs.

And there beside her, lying in a bassinet wrapped up in a swaddling blanket so that only the wisps of jet-black curls on her head poked out above her wrinkled little brown face, was a miracle.

It had been among the hardest things Rihad had ever done, to step aside and let a woman he barely trusted walk across a room to do this work that only she could do. After that scene in the palace, she'd been rushed to the hospital, where the finest doctors in the kingdom had assured them that while the baby was coming a bit early, that didn't mean anything was wrong with either it or Rihad's new bride. And sure enough, when Sterling's exquisitely formed little daughter entered the world at last, she was perfect in every respect. Tiny, perhaps, but utterly, undeniably perfect.

Rihad had been there moments later, to see a woman he'd dismissed as nothing more than callous and calculating beaming down at the scrap of a girl she held in her arms, the look on her face so intimate, so filled with love, it had almost been too much to bear.

He'd had the strangest sensation then—the oddest regret. As if she really was meant to be his. As if this was meant to be his family in more than simply name. As if this was all wrong, somehow—that he should have been there with her, holding her hand, reminding her she wasn't alone, sharing his strength so hers would seem that much more boundless. Not an intruder into these first moments between mother and child, but a part of it. That was all insane, of course. He'd tried to shake it off as he'd approached her, stiff and formal.

She'd glanced up at him, and that look on her face had altered. That wasn't a surprise, but still, Rihad had felt it like a blow. Her mouth had flattened when she'd seen him. She'd hidden that naked joy in her gaze.

He'd hated it.

"Her name is Leyla," Sterling had told him after a moment, as if she'd needed a breath or two to pull herself together before she could speak.

There had been nurses bustling in and out of the birthing suite behind him, doctors being paged incessantly from the intercom out in the corridor, but Sterling had been still. Rihad had had the notion that she'd been waiting for some kind of strike. From him.

As well she should, he'd thought.

It had made that sensation of inexplicable loss yawn open even wider within him. The baby had made tiny noises, more a creaking sound than actual crying, and Sterling had finally relented, her mouth curving into a sweet little smile as she looked down to soothe the little girl that almost undid him. When she'd looked up again, it had almost killed him. He'd never seen that expression on her face before, not even in those happy tabloid pictures of her and Omar. Open. Loving. Soft.

Something like pure.

Even then, at such a tender moment that had nothing at all to do with him, Rihad had wondered what it would be like if that look had been meant for him—and then he'd wondered if he'd utterly lost his mind.

Not if so much as when, he'd told himself then.

"It was Omar's favorite name for a girl," she'd continued after a moment, a faint line appearing between her brows. "That's not… I mean, is there some royal naming tradition I should know about?"

"No." He'd sounded so stiff. So altered. "Leyla is a lovely name."

"She's wonderful," Sterling had whispered then, bending her face back down to the infant, fierce and maternal—and he'd had to leave. Because he hadn't known what to do with that roaring, howling thing inside of him, so threaded through with emotions he didn't know how to process.

Emotions he hardly recognized. What had emotions ever had to do with his life before now? His was a cool world, rational and logical and coldly reasoned. It was his weapon, his strength. The bedrock of his ability to rule his country. He didn't know what the hell to do with all these *feelings*. He didn't know what it made him, that he felt anything at all for this woman or her child. He didn't know what he was supposed to *do* with any of it.

He'd waited until night fell before he returned, and he slipped in only after his security detail assured him she slept at last. He told himself a thousand different reasons why that was the proper, even respectful, thing to do for a woman he hardly knew who'd just given birth—but the truth was, he was completely off balance and he knew it. He wasn't sure he knew *himself*, was the thing—as if he'd been a stranger to himself since Sterling had walked up to him outside that building half a world away. And that alone was enough to give him pause.

Enough to keep him standing there in the shadows.

The child moved in her swaddling then, making that tiny noise again. Part alien, he thought, and part feline, and still it tugged at him. Rihad moved over to the bassinet before he knew he meant to leave his post across the room, seating himself in the chair beside it.

"Hush, little one," he murmured, stroking his fingers down the whisper-soft plushness of one newborn cheek, marveling at it as he did. "Let your mother sleep."

Then he covered the baby's soft little body with his hand, letting the warmth of his palm seep into the rounded swell of her tiny belly, and sure enough, she quieted. Just as he'd done for his half sister Amaya when she'd been an infant. Just as he remembered watching his mother do to baby Omar when Rihad had been a small boy.

Rihad stayed where he was, gazing down at her sweet face, all those dark curls and the eyes that he'd seen earlier were a liquid black that reminded him of his brother, and tried to make sense of the wild tumult within him.

Like an earthquake, when he knew he wasn't moving and neither was the ground beneath him. It tore him apart even so, even while he felt little Leyla's sweet new breaths beneath his hand.

Or perhaps it was because of her.

And he'd been furious for such a long time now. He'd been in a dark, black, consuming rage since he'd gotten that call from the Parisian police. Since he'd had to bury his younger brother so many years before his time. He'd understood it was grief, mixed up somewhere in that terrible rage inside of him, but understanding such a thing hadn't done much to soothe him or stop the fury. His anger—that Omar had been lost so tragically, at this woman who had twisted him into unrecognizable pieces, at the marriage he'd felt he had no choice but to insist upon no matter how little he might have wished it—had been a living flame, hotter by the day, and he'd stopped wondering when or if it might go out.

It had been so easy to focus it all on Sterling. His brother's whore, Rihad's new wife—

But here, now, it was gone. Extinguished completely.

That was what he felt, Rihad realized then. That internal earthquake ripped away his fury and left him with no one to blame. There was only the darkness of fate, the sheer, spinning horror that was his brother's pointless, untimely death.

And this tiny, perfect child was all that remained of Omar on this earth. This little scrap of life, so new she still bore the wrinkles from the womb, was all that was left of the brother Rihad had only ever wished to protect, from his own debauchery as from anything else.

"I will not fail with you, little one," he vowed then. "No matter what."

And it was only when he spoke that he felt the dampness of water on his face. He made no move to wipe it away. Not here in this dark place where no one could see him. Where he could not see himself. Where there was nothing but his grief and this brand-new life he held in his hands.

He felt stretched out taut between the two, the dark and the light. Perhaps he always would.

"I will not fail you again, brother," he whispered into the night. To Omar, wherever he was now. To the little baby that was all that remained of his brother. To the woman his brother had held above his own family, however little Rihad might understand that. None of that mattered any longer. "I will not fail the family you left behind. This I swear."

* * *

Sterling woke that first night again and again, jolted awake by some internal panic that had her jackknifing up in her bed in alarm each time. But she found Leyla right there beside her, more beautiful each time she kissed her sweet cheeks or held her surprisingly hot little body against her own skin.

Those first days were a blurry sort of cartwheel through time, when all she could see or hear or focus on at all was this perfect little creature she'd somehow been chosen to bring into the world, and the astonishingly steep learning curve required to take care of her as she deserved—even in the Bakrian palace, where she had all the help she needed. That didn't alter the weight of the responsibility she felt to this creature she found she loved bigger and wider and better than she'd imagined it was possible to love anything.

Her world shrank down to Leyla, only Leyla, and through her a connection to Omar again, who felt a little bit less lost to her when she held the daughter they'd made in her arms.

Beyond that, there was nothing save the dark, surprisingly quiet man who kept watch over her in his own way, moving in and out of the periphery of all that wasn't Leyla until Sterling was as close to *used to him* as she imagined anyone could be around a man as intense and nerve-racking as Rihad.

She'd even dreamed she'd seen him in her room while she slept, watching over her like some guardian angel. She knew it was absurd. She'd given up believing in guardian angels a long time ago, and Rihad was more warrior than angel anyway, but the notion was warming all the same. It made her feel something like safe—and perhaps a woman who hadn't so recently given birth might have questioned that. Investigated her own feelings, looked for reasons why a man like Rihad felt like safety when she knew perfectly well he was anything but.

As it was, Sterling merely accepted it, forgot about it, and kept her attention on Leyla.

Who, despite that unfurling of love and hope that had swamped Sterling from the moment she'd first seen her, was not gaining the weight she should have in those crucial first days. And for the first three weeks of her life, it was nothing but panic and worry and a terrible battle, no sleep and too many tears, as Sterling tried to breastfeed her and failed.

Again and again, she failed.

All she'd ever wanted was a family of her own, a child she would treat far better than she'd ever been treated herself, and now that Leyla was here she couldn't even manage to *feed* her.

When Rihad found her in the chair next to her bed in her suite in the palace, finally bottle-feeding Leyla on the express and stern orders of the palace's physician, Sterling had finally given up. She couldn't remember the last time she'd taken a shower, or felt like anything but a great, gristled knot of pain and failure.

Everything hurt. Everywhere. Inside and out. Her battered body and her beat-up heart alike.

But her baby girl, who hadn't managed to get anything from Sterling's own breast, was finally feeding hungrily. Almost gleefully. It should have made her feel better, to see that Leyla was obviously going to be fine now that she was able to eat her fill. It did, in a very deep and fundamental way that told her things about how limited her own parents had been.

Yet that had nothing to do with why Sterling was sobbing. Broken into a thousand pieces. Shaking as she held the bottle to Leyla's busy mouth.

"Why are you crying?" Rihad asked, but in a very nearly gentle tone, unlike anything she'd ever heard from him—which might have set off an alarm or two somewhere inside of her, had she had room to process such things. "Has something happened?"

"Are you here to gloat?" she hurled back at him, tears streaming down her face unchecked because her arms were full of baby and bottle, self-recrimination and regret. "Call me more names? Comment on what a mess I am? How toxic a spill I am now, as you predicted?"

And then she was shocked almost out of her skin when the high and mighty King of Bakri simply reached over and took the baby from her with a matter-of-fact confidence that suggested he'd done exactly that a whole lot more often than Sterling ever had. He held Leyla in the crook of his arm and the bottle in his other hand as competently as any of the nurses who'd been in and out these past weeks. He leaned back against the side of the high bed, held the bottle to the baby's sweet mouth and fixed his arrogant stare on Sterling once Leyla started suckling enthusiastically once again.

"What names do you imagine I should call you?" he asked mildly. "Do you have new ones in mind or will the old ones do? You seem to recall them so clearly."

Sterling pulled her legs up beneath her, hugged her knees to her chest in the shapeless, ugly pajamas she'd been wearing for a long time and felt split wide-open with guilt and grief and intense self-loathing.

"Selfish, vain, I don't know." Nothing he could call her was worse than what she was calling herself just then. "If I was any kind of real woman, real mother, I would be able to do the most natural thing in the world, wouldn't I?"

"Give birth?" He sounded completely unemotional, which was maybe why she was able to talk about this at all. The doctor had been so sympathetic it had made Sterling want to scream, then collapse to the floor in a puddle. She didn't want sympathy. She wanted to know *why*. She wanted to know *exactly how much* she was to blame and *precisely how correct* her foster parents had been when they'd assured her she wasn't worthy of a real family. "I believe you already did that, and quite well, if this child is any indication."

Sterling rubbed her palms over her face, somewhat surprised to find herself shaking. "That was the easy part."

"I've never done it myself, I grant you." His voice was so arid then that it made her tears dry up in response. "But I think it's a commonly held truth that while labor is undoubtedly many things, *easy* is not one of them."

"There was an entire hospital wing's worth of doctors and nurses right there, advising me and guiding me. I could have been knocked out and they would have done the whole thing without my input or participation." She knew she was being ridiculous, could tell from the way she felt almost seasick where she sat when she knew she wasn't moving—but that didn't change the way she felt. What she *knew*. She'd told Omar she couldn't do this, much less without him, and here was the proof. "This is what *I* needed to do, all by myself. This is what I'm *supposed* to do and I can't do it."

He didn't respond, that fierce, brooding attention of his on the baby in his arms again—the baby who looked as if she could be his, she realized with a distant sort of jolt. That same rich brown skin, those same fathomless eyes. Because of course a baby of Omar's would look as if she belonged to Rihad, as well. Why hadn't she expected the family resemblance? Another kind of jolt hit her that she couldn't entirely define, so wrapped up was it in all the rest of that storm inside of her.

"At the very least," she made herself say, because if she didn't she would break into sobs, "I'm exactly the useless, selfish bitch you already think I am."

"What I think," Rihad said after it seemed her words had crowded out all the air in the room and simply hung there like suffocating proclamations of inescapable truths, "is that it would be profoundly selfish indeed to continue to try to do something that isn't working, against all medical advice, when surely the only goal here is to feed the child. No matter how you manage it."

"But everybody knows—" she began, almost angrily, because she wanted to believe him more than she could remember wanting anything else, and yet she couldn't let herself off the hook. She simply couldn't.

They'd told her all those years ago that she was worthless. Useless. She'd always suspected they were right—

"I was exclusively bottle-fed, as was Omar," Rihad said then, smooth and inexorable, his dark brows edging high in a kind of regal challenge. "Our mother never intended to breast-feed either one of us. She never did.

And no one ever dared suggest that the Queen of Bakri was anything less than a woman, I assure you. Moreover, I seem to have turned out just fine." His voice was still so dry, and when she only stared back at him, and her tears became salt against her cheeks, he laughed. "You preferred Omar, I understand. But he, too, was a product of the bottle, Sterling."

Sterling let out a long, slow breath and felt it shudder all the way out, as if she'd picked up a great deal more than simply the baby when he strode in here, and stood there holding all of it off her for the first time in weeks. Maybe that was why she didn't police herself the way she should have. That and the unwieldy mess of guilt and fear and worry that there was something bent and twisted, something rotten that would ruin her child, too, careening around inside of her.

"I want to be a good mother," she whispered desperately, as if this man was her priest. As if he really was as safe as he felt just now. "I have to be a good mother to her."

Because of Omar, yes. Because she owed him that. But it was more than that now. It was also because her own mother had been so useless, so remarkably unequal to the task of having a child. Because Sterling had once been a baby called Rosanna whom everyone had discarded.

And because everything had changed.

She'd been forced across the planet and into a marriage with the last man on earth she'd ever wanted to meet, much less marry. But then she'd given birth to this squalling, angry-faced, tiny demon thing with alien eyes and that fragile little head covered in all those dark curls, and everything had simply…shifted.

She felt twice as big on the inside than she could ever be on the outside, ripped open and wholly altered by a kind of glorious light she hadn't known could exist. Love, maybe. Hope. Both.

As if windows she hadn't known were inside of her had been tossed wide-open, and nothing but sunshine streamed in.

And she'd known the instant she'd held her baby against her own skin that she absolutely had to be a good mother to this little girl. To her daughter. No matter what that meant. No matter what it took.

Her eyes met Rihad's then, over Leyla's dark little head and soft brown cheeks. This man who detested her, who had never thought she was anything but the worst kind of whore, and had said so. And Rihad's dark brows edged up that fine, fierce forehead of his even farther, as if he was astonished that she was in any doubt following his stated opinion on the matter.

It occurred to her that there was something the matter with her, that she should find that so comforting.

"You are a good mother," he replied.

It sounded like one of his royal decrees. And Sterling wanted to believe that, too. Oh, how she wanted to believe it.

"You can't know that," she argued, her palm moving to rub against that ache in her chest she didn't understand, in the very place where Leyla's hot head had first rested. She scowled at him instead, because it was easier. "And the fact I can't nurse my own child certainly suggests otherwise."

"This is the great beauty of living in a monarchy, Sterling." His lips twitched, which on anyone else she might have called the beginnings of a smile, or even laughter—but this was Rihad. "The only opinion on the subject—on any subject, in fact—that matters at all is mine. Are you not relieved? If I say you are an excellent mother, that is not merely a social nicety I am extending to my brand-new wife on a trying afternoon for her. It is an edict, halfway to a law."

"But—"

"Go," he ordered her. He lifted his chin in that commanding way of his when she only blinked back at him as if he'd lapsed into Arabic. "Take a shower. A bath. A walk outside. Sleep as much as possible and let others worry about this one. She will be fine, even if you let her out of your sight. This I promise."

Leyla hadn't been out of Sterling's reach since her birth. Not even once. "But I can't—"

"This is the royal palace," he reminded her gently. Yet still with that implacable steel beneath his words. "I am perfectly capable of watching an infant but I don't have to do that, either, because we have an extensive and very well-paid nursing staff here to tend to her every possible need. Which you might have noticed over the past three weeks had you not been so determined to drive yourself into the ground."

"But—"

"Martyrdom is actually a far less endearing trait than many people seem to imagine, Sterling. And it always ends the same unpleasant and painful way." His voice was all steel again then, and dark command besides. "Let the nurses do their jobs."

"I don't need them," she argued, though she was so tired she thought she might fall off into sleep right where she sat, if she let herself. As if sleep was a cliff and she'd been balancing on the edge of it for weeks now, unsteadily. "Leyla is *my* daughter."

"Leyla is also a royal princess of the House of Bakri," Rihad said, with all that innate power of his she hadn't forgotten, exactly, but had certainly stopped noting in the past few weeks. There was no noting anything else then, not when he sounded like that—as if he truly was issuing edicts he expected her to follow. "There is nothing, no accommodation or luxury or whim, that is not available to her at a moment's notice."

His dark gold gaze moved over hers, seeing things Sterling feared she was too tired to hide the way she should. And she was definitely suffering from sleep deprivation, she told herself, because there was no way Rihad would actually look at her the way he seemed to be then, with an expression that veered far too close to tenderness.

But that was impossible. She was delirious.

"You do not have to do this by yourself, Sterling," he said quietly. "Especially not here in the royal palace. I don't know what you think you have to prove."

She knew exactly what she felt she had to prove, but she couldn't tell him. She couldn't tell anyone, but she especially couldn't tell Rihad—and not only, she assured herself, because this was the nicest, warmest interaction she'd had with the man since she'd met him. But also because he wasn't her confidante. He was her husband, yes, but only in the broadest sense of the term. There was no relationship, no trust. There wasn't even affection, despite that odd light she'd imagined in his gaze just then. There was no intimacy.

Only that one kiss, she thought, the memory prickling over and into her, like gooseflesh rising along her arms. She'd almost forgotten it.

Perhaps she'd wanted to forget it, as there was no making sense of it.

She shoved it away again now, as his too-incisive gaze rested on hers as if he was also reliving those strange, wild moments with his mouth hard on hers. She needed sleep, that was all. Especially before she started thinking about things that made no sense—things she'd been so certain were purely hormonal and would disappear when she was no longer pregnant.

Maybe that kiss was still something she needed to sleep on, she thought then, as a different sort of shiver moved through her. Maybe it was something she needed *at least* a long shower and a good night's rest to consider. Or maybe it was better by far—safer, certainly—to pretend it had never happened.

But either way Sterling stopped arguing and did as he'd told her.

Carrying that image, of the ruthless and terrible Rihad al Bakri cradling her tiny infant daughter in his strong arms, from the long, hot shower and straight on into her dreams.

CHAPTER SIX

"I OWE YOU an apology, Rihad," Sterling said, her voice crisp and matter-of-fact.

She'd worked hard to make it that way. To sound businesslike, which suited this strange marital arrangement of theirs instead of actually apologetic, which did not. *Apologetic* was far too emotional.

They sat out in the fantastical garden that was the king's private retreat in the center of the palace. Lush plants tangled with brightly colored flowers around three separate fountains, while gentle canopies covered the different seating areas tucked into this little bit of wilderness hidden away inside the palace complex. It was possibly the most beautiful thing Sterling had ever seen.

Then again, so was Rihad—not that it was at all smart to let herself think along those lines.

It's like admiring the tapestries in my suite, she told herself today, sitting across from him at the graceful iron table where their breakfast had been laid out for them, the way it was every summer morning. *That he's beautiful is a fact, not an emotional thing at all, and certainly doesn't take away from how terrible he always was to Omar.*

But when he glanced up from the tablet computer where he'd been scrolling through something the way he often did, she felt too hot and looked away, and only partially because his dark gold gaze seemed harsher than usual today. She looked toward the nearest fountain that had been made to resemble a tropical waterfall, gurgling down over slick, shiny rocks to form a small, inviting pool Rihad had once told her she was welcome to make use of whenever she wished.

Yet somehow, despite the fact this man had seen her at her worst, dirty and crazy and sobbing and wild, the idea of him seeing her in anything like a bathing suit—splashing around in front of him or, worse, with him—made her heart thud too hard inside her chest. She chose to ignore that, the way she always did.

She ignored more and more by the day, she knew. And it was only getting worse.

They had taken to having their meals together here in the weeks since Rihad had forcibly removed Leyla from her arms and insisted Sterling take care of herself. Well. It was more that Rihad had decreed that they would take their meals here, whenever it was possible with his schedule, and Sterling hadn't had it in her to object.

You didn't want to object, a voice deep inside of her whispered. *Or you would have.*

"It seems I must keep an eye on you," he'd said when he'd informed her of this new schedule. She'd been fresh from her first full night of sleep since Leyla's birth and had felt drunk with it. Like a different person.

And he had looked at her in a way that had made her breath catch, as if he'd truly wanted nothing more than to take care of her. As if he really was some kind of guardian angel—though she knew better. She did.

Life had shifted all around her in these strange months since Leyla's birth, then settled into a new form altogether. Sterling slept well at last. She spent her days with the baby and the fleet of cheerful, efficient nurses Rihad had acquired and who made Sterling feel like twice the mother she suspected she was. She took long walks around the palace and the surrounding grounds and gardens, sometimes pushing Leyla's buggy and sometimes on her own, enjoying how much more like herself she felt by the day.

How oddly content she felt, here in her forced marriage to a man she'd vowed years ago to hate forever, no matter if Omar had or not. She'd been happy to carry that torch. She'd meant it on their wedding day when she'd told Rihad she hated him.

And then you kissed him.

But she didn't want to think about that.

The presence of the nurses meant she had time to read again, to exchange emails with her friends in New York, to reacquaint herself with the life she'd put on hold when Omar had died. She started to imagine what might come next for her. She got back in touch with the foundation she'd worked with to aid foster children once they aged out of the system and found in the various responses to her marriage that things were very different now.

Omar's friends, perhaps predictably, felt betrayed.

I understand why you'd feel that way, she emailed one after the next, trying hard to hold on to her patience—because where had they all been when she'd tried to run from Rihad? They'd texted, yes. Called. But not one of them had actually shown up that morning to help a heavily pregnant woman escape her fate.

Her entire plan had been to disappear somewhere and hope for the best. That had worked out well enough when she'd been fifteen and on her own—or in any case, she'd survived—but would it have been fair to Leyla? Sterling might have been married against her will, but a little bit of distance and a whole lot more sleep had made her think that having Leyla's future assured was what mattered. That it was the *only* thing that mattered—and no matter that it was Omar's infamously judgmental brother who'd made that possible.

But give me some credit, she'd chided Omar's old friends—*her* old friends, too, not that anyone seemed to remember that while busy picking sides. *Leyla is a princess and Bakri is a part of her birthright she can only access if legitimate. That's all this marriage is: legitimacy for Leyla.*

The charities and foundations she'd worked with who'd known her as Omar's lover, by contrast, were *ecstatic* at the notion of working with the Queen of Bakri—a title Sterling hadn't fully realized was hers to claim now.

Maybe a little bit too ecstatically, she'd thought only that morning, when yet another solicitation had hit her inbox.

It was only then that she realized that Rihad was staring at her across the table, and that she had no idea how much time had passed since she'd last spoken.

"Why are you looking at me like that?"

"You told me you wished to apologize and then lapsed into silence," he replied, mildly enough—though once again, there was a gleam in the dark gold of his gaze that reminded her what a dangerous man he was. That suggested he was *waiting* for something as he watched her. "I thought perhaps you were rendered mute by the enormity of your sins."

"My sins have been widely overexaggerated, I think." It had been two months since that kiss she found herself thinking about much more than she should. It was something about his mouth, crooked slightly in that sardonic way of his that thudded through her. "I wanted to apologize for falling apart the way I did in the first place. It's taken me weeks to realize just how out of it I was."

Rihad shifted in his seat, his strong fingers toying with the steaming cup of rich coffee before him on the table. And though the baby slept happily in her little buggy beside Sterling's chair, Sterling had the sudden, crazy desire to wake her up—so there would be something else to concentrate on, something other than the way this lethal man was looking at her. A distraction from all of this intensity that swirled between them like the desert heat itself.

"And here I thought your apology would be for telling all your American friends that our marriage was a fake."

She blinked. "What?"

A deeper, darker crook of that mouth. "I think you heard me."

"Yes, but..." Had he been reading her email? But even if he had been, and she wasn't sure she'd put it past him, she'd never said that. Never quite that. "I never said that. Not to anyone."

"Were you misquoted, then?" He slid his tablet computer across the table to her. "Show me where, and I will notify my attorneys at once."

Sterling swiped her finger across the screen and

stared down at the page that opened before her, from a famously snide tabloid paper.

Queen of the Rebound screamed the headline. Then beneath it:

Sexy Sterling uses famous wiles to bewitch Omar's grieving brother, the King of Bakri, but tells pals back home: "This marriage is for Baby Leyla. It's all for show."

The worst part, Sterling thought as she glared down at the offensive article and felt her stomach drop to her feet, was that she had no idea *which* of the people she'd thought were her friends had betrayed her.

"You understand that this is problematic, do you not?" he asked, still in that mild tone—though she was starting to see that there were other truths in that hard gleam in his eyes, in the tense way he held that mouth-watering body of his as he sat there in one of those dark suits of his that some artist of a tailor had crafted to perfectly flatter every hard plane, every ripple of muscle. Every inch of sensual male threat that emanated from him, made worse because of the luxurious trappings.

"It's a tabloid," she said dismissively, because she might note that threat in him but for some reason, it didn't frighten her. Quite the opposite. "It's their job to be problematic. It's our job to ignore them."

"I would ordinarily agree with you," Rihad said, so reasonably that she almost nodded along, almost lulled by his tone despite the way her pulse leaped in her veins. "But this is a delicate situation."

She deliberately misunderstood him, sliding the tablet back toward him and returning her attention to the selection of fruit and thick yogurt, flaky pastries and strong coffee, as if that was the most important thing she could possibly concentrate on just then: her breakfast. And so what if she wasn't hungry?

"This is tabloid nonsense, nothing more," she said, as calmly as she could. "Nothing delicate about it, I'm afraid. They like to smash at things until they break, then claim they were broken all along. Surely you know this."

He didn't speak for a moment and she tried to pretend that didn't get to her—but eventually she couldn't help herself and glanced up again, to find Rihad watching her too closely with a narrow sort of gaze, as if he was trying to puzzle her out.

She swallowed hard, and she couldn't tell if it was because she wanted to keep her secrets hidden from him, or if she wanted to lay them all out before him in a gesture so suicidal it should have traumatized her even to imagine it. Yet somehow, it didn't.

"The whole world knows that Leyla is Omar's daughter, not mine, no matter that my name is on her birth certificate," he said, after a moment, when she was beginning to imagine she might simply crack open.

"Did I know that you put your name on the birth certificate?" Sterling asked, shocked and taken aback, somehow, at that little revelation. "I don't think I did."

She remembered his look of dark impatience, though she hadn't seen it in a while. That made it all the more effective today.

"Exactly what sort of legitimacy did you imagine I meant to convey on your child when I married you?"

"I guess the sort where we're not completely erasing Omar from his daughter's life." She reached over and fiddled with the hem of the blanket that drooped over the side of the buggy, though Leyla still slept soundly and no adjustments were needed.

"It is a legal maneuver, nothing more," Rihad said, his tone harsher than it had been in months, but that couldn't be why her chest felt tight. It shouldn't matter to her either way. "But you're making my point for me. Omar has not been erased in any meaningful way. Everyone knows who fathered Leyla. Her place might be assured on paper and in the courts, but in the eyes of the Bakrian people and, more important, our enemies, her legitimacy must come from us."

"Us?"

"Us. Me, their king, and you, my brand-new and deeply controversial queen."

She shied away from that term, scowling at him instead. "I don't like that word."

"Which one?" His voice was so dry then. So dark and compelling. *Us? Controversial?*

"Queen." Her scowl deepened. "It's ridiculous. It doesn't fit the situation at all."

She meant it didn't fit *her*, trash dressed up in an unearned crown—and she had the strangest notion he knew exactly what she meant. His dark gold gaze almost hurt against hers.

"And yet it is your title, accorded to you with all due deference two months ago when you married the King of Bakri. That would be me, in case you're not following this conversation, willfully or otherwise."

"But I don't want to be your—"

"Enough," Rihad said then, cutting her off.

He sat back in his chair, never shifting those mesmerizing eyes of his from hers, looking dark and terrible and entirely too fascinating, from that brusque nose of his to his strong jaw and all that rich brown skin in between. She wanted to lean closer to him, explore him—and hated herself.

"I don't care what you call yourself, Sterling. You are my queen either way. I suggest you accept it." When she didn't respond, that light in his gaze sharpened and made it a little too hard to breathe. "I think you understand perfectly well that we cannot allow any speculation that this marriage is fake to fester. It serves no one but our enemies."

She felt oddly fragile. "Why do you keep talking about enemies?"

"The kingdom has been rocked by one scandal after the next and we are weak." His gaze sharpened. "My father's tumultuous love affairs. My wife's death without giving me any heirs. Omar's notorious mistress that he flaunted in the tabloids and his refusal to come back home and do his duty. My sister's betrothal to Kavian of Daar Talaas, which she responded to by running away—"

"I like her already."

"Amaya was a successful runaway, Sterling. She's managed to avoid both my security and Kavian's for months. Kavian will no doubt run out of patience with her, and when he does? Our countries will not unite and if they do not, Bakri will fall. There are too many other powers in the area that want our location and our shipping prowess, and we cannot possibly keep them all at bay alone."

"You're talking about *your* enemies." She lifted her

chin as she held that harsh gaze of his. "The only enemy I've ever been aware of was you."

"I am talking about *our* enemies." He nodded toward the tablet. "Or do you imagine that whatever 'pal' sold that story is your friend? Will they take you in when I am imprisoned and you—if you are lucky—are a royal Bakrian in exile?"

Sterling opened her mouth to argue when something else occurred to her. That wild kiss swelled up in her again, a tactile memory. Searing through her as if it had only just happened. Flooding her with sensory images, with yearning, all over again.

"Is this really because you're worried about how our marriage is perceived?" she asked him. "Because of *enemies*? Or is it because you want to get into my pants?"

He didn't move a muscle. She knew that because she was watching him so closely that she could see it when he breathed. He didn't even tense. And yet he seemed to explode outward, becoming twice his size and a thousand times more dangerous, like some kind of mystical being let loose from its cage at last.

And every single cell in Sterling's body shivered to red alert.

She was flushed with the heat of it. Her skin seemed to ache for his touch. Her breasts felt too heavy and the taut peaks pulled tight. Inside of her, there was a low, hot humming that coiled between her legs and pulsed. Hard and wet. Ready.

It was the most carnal experience of her entire life.

It was the *only* carnal experience she'd ever had, save that last kiss.

And they weren't even touching.

* * *

That he did not turn over the table between them and taste her again right now was, Rihad thought, the only evidence remaining that he had once been a civilized man.

He thought too much about his enemies as it was. He did not want to think about Sterling's pants. He did not want to think about that body of hers that had re-defined grace while heavily pregnant and now... She was difficult to look away from.

He found he rarely did.

Rihad did not want to think about the way he fought himself to keep from touching her, because he was de-termined to make this marriage work in some fashion or another, the way it had with his first wife. He and Tas-nim had been friends, after a fashion. They'd eased into the physical aspects of their marriage and had worked on their friendship first. He'd decided at some point during the first days of gorgeous little Leyla's life that he owed her mother no less, no matter how they'd come to find themselves married.

But that did not explain why he took himself in hand each morning in his shower to slake his growing need. And it certainly did not explain the tempting array of images he tortured himself with as he did so.

His voice was quiet when he finally answered her, and it cost him. "Can't I be preoccupied with both the perception of our marriage *and* 'getting in your pants,' as you so charmingly put it?"

"Unlikely. Men are more often focused on the one thing above all else."

"That shows how little you know me. I am not merely a man. I am a king."

"I know you enough, Your Majesty."

Her blue eyes rivaled the summer sun above them, and yet even when she looked straight at him he was certain he could *see* the walls she kept up, high and bolstered. He loathed them more and more each day. He wanted them knocked down. And he was entirely too aware that the urge was not exactly *friendly*.

"And besides," she continued, her voice light, "you don't really want into these pants anyway." She let out a self-deprecating laugh and waved her free hand in the general direction of her midsection. "Everything's gone a little crazy after giving birth."

He snorted. "Self-deprecation does not suit you, Sterling."

She frowned at him, and he saw her ball her hands into fists, then drop them in her lap. "I don't know what that means."

"It means you were gifted with the sort of genetics that make most women green with envy, as I suspect you are aware." He shifted in his chair and let his gaze move all over her, which was not exactly an improvement for that wild hunger battering at him from within. Because she had been so beautiful when they'd met that she'd made Manhattan disappear so he could better admire her. And she grew more beautiful by the day. And the fact that she was no longer big with her pregnancy was the least part of that. "You gained a minimal amount of weight while carrying Leyla, lost most of it while giving birth to her and are probably healthier now than when you got pregnant in the first place. If the fashionably gaunt pictures I've seen of you back then are any guide."

He saw emotions he couldn't name flit across her face, one after the next, and he hated that he couldn't read them. Or her. That she defied him even now, without a single word, by simple virtue of remaining opaque.

Rihad couldn't have said when he'd begun to find that intolerable.

"I'll thank you to keep your comments on my body to yourself."

He smiled, and then wider when he saw the spray of goose bumps rise along her bare arms. "Unfortunately for you, Sterling, you are mine. And I take a keen interest in the welfare of the things that belong to me, whether that means trade prospects in my cities or my wife's form."

She was flushed, he noted, and he was sure that if he mentioned it she would claim it was disgust. Distress. But he didn't believe that.

"How delightfully medieval."

And he enjoyed this, Rihad realized with a thud. He *liked* her sharp tone, her icy wit, even if it was at his expense. Because Sterling was the only person he'd ever met who dared speak to him this way.

Perhaps there was something wrong with him after all, that he should enjoy it—*her*—so much.

"Your body is fine, Sterling," he told her, as much to see her draw herself up in outrage as anything else. He made a show of drinking from his coffee cup, then setting it down, for the sheer pleasure of watching temper crack through those blue eyes of hers like lightning. "You're not a model any longer. You certainly don't need to keep yourself so drawn and skeletal." He smiled again, and he could feel the wolf in it. "If you want to dissuade me from making advances on you, you'll have to come up with something better than that."

Her lips quivered and her gaze flashed dark, with

something he didn't understand. He was fascinated all the same.

"How about this." Her voice was fierce, almost aggressive, but that only deepened his fascination. "Don't make advances on me at all. I don't want you."

He watched her for a moment. He waited, and sure enough, she flushed again, brighter and delightfully redder than before.

"Now, that's just an outright lie," he murmured.

And she looked away, because he was right. And she hated it. And he loved that he could read *that* as easily as the text on his tablet.

"Is this where you force me again?" she asked tightly, her eyes on the pool nearest the table while her body shouted out all the ways she was a liar, again and again, as if it was in collusion with Rihad. "Because that was so much fun when you called it a wedding."

He laughed then and saw her jolt with surprise. She turned back to him, her gaze unreadable again, but he'd come to a decision. The *friendship* angle had been fine these past months. It had been appropriate. The woman had just had another man's child—and lost that man to a tragic accident besides. But it was time to move on.

Rihad stood, aware of the way her eyes clung to him as he moved, very much as if she was finding his body as much a temptation as he found hers.

"We'll have a honeymoon, I think," he said, and watched her shift restlessly in her chair, the truth in the pink bloom on her cheeks. "You and me for two weeks in the desert, with a thousand opportunities for intimacy."

"What?" She sounded panicked, and he was not a

civilized creature, he realized. Not at all, because he liked that. "Intimacy? Why would you want that?"

"Perception." He shrugged. "Of course, it will be widely assumed that you're merely pandering to my base, animal instincts with that famously lush body of yours. Men are beasts, are they not? And I am no better than my brother when it comes to your seductive powers."

"Yes, you are!" Sterling looked alarmed. "You live to resist me! Or you should."

"I am unfamiliar with weakness," he told her, and he didn't care if that truth hit her as arrogance. It didn't make it any less true. "But in this case, succumbing to the practiced charms of a known seductress is a weakness I am prepared to allow the world to dissect at their leisure." He eyed her aghast expression. "Doesn't that sound like a wonderful story for your tabloid-loving friends to sell far and wide?"

Her voice was scratchy when she answered, and her eyes were much too bright with a heat he wanted to bathe himself in. "It sounds heinous. And completely unbelievable anyway."

"Why don't you ask me the question?" He thrust his hands into the pockets of his trousers, because he doubted she'd appreciate it if he put them on her. Yet.

"Why are you so awful?" Sterling asked at once, her voice sharp but with that storm in her blue eyes. "But I already know the answer, of course. Because you can be."

"That's not the question you want to ask."

Sterling stared back at him. He heard the summer breeze high above them, dancing through the plants and the trees, and the running water all around them, like songs. He saw her pulse hammer against the delicate skin of her neck and wanted nothing more than to press his mouth to it, as if he could taste her excitement. He saw her hands open and then bunch into fists again, as if she couldn't control them.

She sat up straighter. Squared her shoulders. Tilted up her chin.

"So we'll simply go out to the desert for a little while. Spend the time out there so people think…whatever they want to think. Call it a honeymoon so the whole world leaps to the same conclusion. That we're together in more ways than one. A unit."

"Yes."

She swallowed, hard. "You won't… I mean, we won't…"

"I have no intention of forcing you to consummate this marriage," he said bluntly, and he told himself it wasn't fair to think she should already know that he was not that kind of man. It didn't help when she sagged in her chair in exaggerated relief. "Have I given you cause to imagine otherwise?"

"You kidnapped me," she pointed out, though what he noticed was how little heat there was in it. "You married me against my will. You'll forgive me if I'm not entirely certain where you draw that line."

He took his time moving around the table. Her eyes widened, but stayed fast to his, and she made a squeaking sort of noise that reminded him of Leyla when he pulled her chair out from the table and then around to face him, so he could brace himself on its arms and put his face directly into hers.

And God help him, but it was sweet.

"Bringing you to Bakri and marrying you before you bore a royal Bakrian child outside of wedlock was my duty," he told her, dark and serious, though he was far more fascinated by the high color on her cheeks than was wise. "Containing the scandal that you represent is my responsibility. But what happens between us now?"

"Nothing is happening! There's no *us* for anything to be between!"

He ignored her. "That has nothing to do with duty." Rihad leaned in closer, so close he could have easily tasted that seductive mouth of hers, yet he held himself back. "That has everything to do with need."

"I have no needs," she said, but then she shivered, and Rihad smiled.

"I won't force you, Sterling," he told her with quiet intent. "I won't need to."

She stared back at him. No snappy comeback. No sharp wit. Wide blue eyes and that pulse of hers a wild staccato in her neck. And he wanted her more than he could recall wanting anything, for all that she was a wild card, a loose woman, a problem to be solved. He accepted all of that.

"But first," he said, "it's time to talk about Omar."

CHAPTER SEVEN

STERLING GAPED AT HIM, her head spinning madly at the sudden shift in conversation and her stomach in a new, hard knot.

"You look at me as if you expect me to transform into a monster where I stand," Rihad pointed out with a certain gruffness, almost as if that wounded him. She told herself she was imagining it. "All fangs and claws and evil intent."

"I'm not sure you haven't already done so."

That mouth of his crooked into something not quite a smile. He reached over and tucked a stray tendril of her copper-blond hair behind one ear, and neither one of them moved for a long, shattering instant.

Then he straightened to his full height, but she could still see that steely glint in his dark gold eyes, the potency of his gaze undiminished.

"I am not going to go on a honeymoon, whether real or for show, with a woman whose head is filled with another man, Sterling. It's time you told me about my brother and your relationship with him."

He didn't object when she pushed back the chair and surged to her feet, hurriedly stepping away from him. He only watched her as she went, and that shattering thing between them seemed to expand into a taut, terrible grip around her heart. But she made herself stand straighter.

"I don't think you really want to have that conversation," she told him as evenly as she could. "You're unlikely to hear anything you like."

Sterling wasn't sure she wanted to have it, either. She felt too guilty, too ashamed. No matter what she might have told their friends or herself, this wasn't what Omar would have wanted. He'd left Bakri for a reason. This—all of this, everything that had happened since the accident—was a stark betrayal of the best friend she'd ever had. The only family she'd ever known.

And that fire inside of her, that terrible flame when she looked at Rihad that she didn't know what to do with, was worse.

"This is not the first time you have insinuated that I harmed my brother in some way," Rihad said darkly. "Why? What is your evidence for this?"

She shook her head, as if she could shake him away that easily, and all his questions, too. "Don't act the innocent, Rihad. It isn't a good fit."

"You mistake innocence for intent, I think. It's time to stop talking in circles, Sterling. If you wish to accuse me of something, do it to my face."

He smiled again then, lethally, and she felt it everywhere.

And she'd forgotten this, hadn't she? She'd been lulled into a false sense of security because there'd been nothing in her head but Leyla and he'd been so encouraging, so supportive, since the day she'd been born. They'd eaten their meals together these past months and talked about a thousand things, like any other civilized strangers who happened to be married to each other. Books, art. The cities they'd seen, the places they'd visited, from Cannes to the Seychelles to Patagonia.

She'd learned that he had been a solemn child and an even more serious young man, studious and focused in all things. She'd discovered that he had played a great deal of soccer and the occasional game of rugby all the way through university, but only for sport, as he'd always known his future. His place.

"That must have been nice," she'd said once. Perhaps too wistfully. "To have no doubt what direction you were headed in, no matter what."

He'd eyed her across their dinner and the candles that had lined the table and she'd shivered, though she hadn't been cold.

"Who can say if it was nice or not?" he'd replied after a moment, as if he'd never thought about it before that instant. "It was all I knew."

She'd started to think of this man as something like *pleasant*. She'd started to imagine that this forced-marriage thing might not be quite so terrible after all. But she'd been kidding herself. This was Rihad al Bakri. He was the most dangerous man she'd ever encountered.

How had she allowed herself to forget that?

"Fine," she said staunchly now, telling herself this had always been inevitable. That they had always been heading straight here. "Let's talk about Omar."

Sterling crossed her arms, wishing she didn't feel so compelled to *dress* each time she knew she would see him, including the airy sundress she wore now that felt a bit unequal to the conversation. She told herself fashion and beauty were armor, the way they had been when she'd been a model and the point was to look at

the clothes, not the woman in them. And they were—
but that wasn't the only reason she did it these days.

The depressing truth was that back then she'd liked
to hide in the glare of any spotlight that might have
been focused on her. But here in this far-off palace that
sometimes felt like a dream over these past months,
she *liked* it when he saw her. When he got that gleam
in his dark gold eyes that told her he appreciated what
he saw. Even now.

She had so many reasons to hate herself that Sterling
couldn't understand why she hadn't started overflow-
ing where she stood. Like a backed-up sewer. That was
precisely how she felt, clogged and *wrong*.

"Wonderful." His gaze was so dark. So intense.
"Let's begin with why Omar persisted in his relationship with you across all these years. He defied his family and his country, abandoned his duties and broke
our father's heart into a thousand pieces. That was un-
accountable enough. Yet he never married you, never
claimed you in the eyes of the world. Never stood up
for you in any way when he knew perfectly well his af-
fair with you was scandalous. Not even when you fell
pregnant."

"You're relentless." But she said that as if it was only
to be expected, without any particular heat. "Omar was
the best man I ever knew. The kindest and the bravest.
He stood up for me in ways you can't imagine."

"My imagination is remarkably vivid." His voice
was cool. "Why don't you try me?"

"Maybe Omar and I didn't want to get married,
Rihad." She sighed when he only gazed at her in arrogant disbelief. "Maybe not everyone is as traditional as
you are. In some places, it's the twenty-first century."

"I have no doubt that you and Omar lived a delightfully modern and unconventional life in every possible way, cavorting about New York City in all that marvelous limelight for so many years." He eyed her in a way she didn't much like then. "But your pregnancy should have snapped him back to the reality that, like it or not, he was a Bakrian royal who owed legitimacy to his own child. Why didn't it?"

"Perhaps he assumed you would swoop in like the Angel of Death and sort it all out to suit yourself," she said coolly. Then threw a smile, sharp and icy, back at him. "And look at that. You did."

"Do you think these little games you seem determined to keep playing will distract me from getting your answer, Sterling? They won't, I promise you. Why didn't he marry you?"

His whole bearing had gotten colder and more regal as he stood there, his gaze a demanding thing that beat at her, and she believed him. She believed that he would keep asking that same question, again and again, until she finally answered it. That he would stand here an eternity if that was what it took. That he was like the great desert that surrounded his country on three sides, monolithic and impassable, and deeply treacherous besides.

"He wanted to marry me," Sterling said after a moment. Then she raised her gaze to meet his again and forced herself not to show him any of the emotion that swirled around inside of her. "I refused."

Rihad laughed. Not at all nicely. It set her teeth on edge, as she imagined it had been meant to do, and she had to order herself to unclench her jaw before she broke something.

"Of course you did." His tone then was so dark, so sardonic, it felt like another one of his disturbingly sensual touches inside of her. "He begged you, I imagine, and you nobly rebuffed him, in the vein of all gold diggers and materialistic mistresses across the ages."

He didn't quite roll his eyes. His derisive tone meant he didn't have to. But Sterling felt sharpened all the same then. Honed into some kind of blade by that dismissive tone of his.

"I know it's hard for you to believe, Rihad. I know it flies directly in the face of all the fantasies you have about social-climbing sluts like me. But that doesn't make it any less true. Omar would have married me in a heartbeat. I was the one with reservations."

"The prospect of becoming a Bakrian princess was too onerous for you? It seemed too much of a thankless chore?" There was that lash in his voice then that should have made her crumble, but she only tilted up her chin and glared back at him. "You were already living off him. Why not make it legal and continue to do so forever?"

"You're such a small man, for a king," she said softly, and had the satisfaction of watching his eyes blaze at the insult. This was the man she'd met in New York. This was the man who had sparred with her in that SUV. It was absurd that some part of her thrilled to see him again, as if she'd missed him. "Or maybe all kings are the same. What do I know? Obsessed with all these tiny details, territories and tabloids, that make them what they are. Life is a great deal richer and more complicated than that."

He studied her for a moment, and Sterling stared right back at him. There was something about the way he was looking at her, about the particular quality of that dark temper she could see inhabiting his gorgeous face just then. If he'd been any other man—if *she'd* been any other woman—she'd have thought it was some kind of jealousy.

But that made absolutely no sense.

"Give me one good reason you wouldn't marry my brother," Rihad growled after a moment or two inched by and still they stood there, faced off like enemy combatants. "You are a woman with no family. No support."

Did he know that was a sore spot for her? Or had he scored a lucky hit? Sterling sucked in a breath and hoped against hope he hadn't noticed.

But his dark eyes gleamed. He noticed everything.

"A marriage to Omar would have changed all that. Even were you to eventually divorce, and even if you'd signed away everything ahead of time as our attorneys would have made certain you did, you would always have remained a part of the kingdom. Your child would always be a member of the royal family. Why would a woman like you turn down that kind of security?"

A woman like you. That phrase rolled around and around inside of her, picking up all the mud and grime of all the other people in her life who had said something like that to her. *No one could want a child like you,* her foster parents had told her. *Girls like you are only good for one thing,* her first, sleazy modeling contact had told her. *I should have known a bird like you would land on her feet,* a British photographer friend of Omar's had sneered in an email only yesterday.

Omar had been the only person she'd ever met who had never, ever, put her in that kind of box. Sterling told herself she had to focus. This was about him, not her.

This was about his life—the one he'd wanted to live, not the one his overbearing brother thought he should have lived.

Maybe there wasn't much *a woman like her* could do to a king, but she could certainly defend her best friend.

"You don't know anything about your brother, do you? You never did."

"I'm growing impatient," Rihad growled. "If you want to continue to talk in circles, that's your prerogative. But I will make no promises about my reaction to that. What I can promise you is that you are unlikely to like it very much."

Sterling took a deep breath.

And then she told him Omar's secret. At last.

"Omar was gay."

If Sterling had reached beneath that maddeningly flowy dress she wore and pulled out a gun, then shot it directly into his heart, Rihad could not have been more shocked.

And for a long, tense moment, it felt as if she'd done exactly that.

The report from her statement echoed so loudly it drowned out the world. It made the breezes still, the far-off noise of the palace and the city beyond fade. Even the water in the fountains seemed to run dry for what seemed like a very long time.

Then she laughed, but it was a bitter, accusing sort of sound. It made him feel worse. Like a monster.

"Is that not what you were looking for, Rihad? I'm so sorry. Not everyone lives according to your narrow standards of behavior."

"Explain this to me." He didn't sound like himself. He sounded like some gruff, autocratic mockery of the person he'd thought he was instead. He knew it. He could hear it. But he didn't care. Not at that moment.

She glared at him. "Sometimes, Rihad, when little princes grow up and want to play with others, they don't want to play with the little princesses as much as the—"

"Explain your relationship with him," he snapped.

"This is ridiculous." She rocked back on her heels and scowled at him. "You didn't grow up beneath a rock. I don't have to explain the world to you. You might choose to act as if it hasn't moved on from the Stone Age here, but you know perfectly well that's a choice you're making, not the truth."

"I don't require that you explain the world to me. Only my brother."

He shook his head, frowning, as every conversation he'd ever had with Omar raced through his head, one after the next. Every time Rihad had brought up Sterling, Omar had shrugged it off.

"She is necessary, brother," he'd said. He'd never explained that assertion any further—and Rihad had thought him besotted. Bewitched. Led about by his most sensitive parts by a scandalous woman. It was a tale as old as time. As old as their own father, certainly.

It had never crossed his mind that this notorious woman, this walking sexual fantasy who had been the torment of thousands the world over in those coyly sensual perfume advertisements that had made her name, could possibly have been Omar's beard.

Yet he believed her, and that meant she'd been exactly that, and he'd fallen for it. To the detriment of his own relationship with his brother.

"I think that if you could see the look on your face right now, you would understand why he felt this was necessary," Sterling said coolly. "Omar didn't dare tell you. He hid in plain sight and used one of the oldest tricks in the book." She raised one hand and made the kind of imperious gesture in his direction that made him all but see red. "That exact expression."

"I have no idea what you think you see on my face," he gritted out. "But let me tell you what's behind it. Shock."

She scowled. "There is absolutely nothing wrong—"

"That he didn't tell me," Rihad threw at her. "That he felt he needed to sever his relationship with his own family. That he felt he needed to keep this secret all these years."

"How could he possibly tell you?" she demanded, and he could see how much she'd cared for Omar in that fiercely defensive light in her blue eyes then, and everything inside him tilted. Slid. Because Rihad had only ever wanted to be that kind of support for his brother, and he'd failed him. "The only thing you ever talked to him about was what a disappointment he was. How he had let you down by not racing off to get married and have babies the way you thought he should. Having Leyla was his attempt to pacify you and *I* wouldn't marry *him* because I thought he deserved more from his life. I thought he could do better than living a lie."

"But this is what I do not understand." Rihad raked his hands through his hair and had the odd notion that he was a stranger to himself. If his brother had been an entirely different man than the one he pretended he was, what else could be a lie dressed up like the truth? He felt cut off at his knees. Adrift in the middle of his own palace, where he had always known exactly what and who he was. "Why go to such lengths to live this lie?"

"I haven't gotten the impression that Bakri is renowned for its open-mindedness," Sterling said in that sharp way of hers that he enjoyed a bit less than usual then. "Much less its king. And I've only been here a few months."

"I can understand why he would not wish to tell our father," Rihad said, as if he was talking to himself. In part, he was. "The old man was harsh, despite his own weaknesses. He was of another time."

"Whereas you are the embodiment of the modern age?" Sterling sniffed. "What with the kidnapping and the ranting about legitimacy and your obsession with al Bakri blood. Very progressive."

"He should have come to me."

"It's not up to you to decide how he should have lived his life," she threw at him, that scowl that twisted her face making her more pretty instead of less, somehow. "What he *wanted* was to live as he pleased. What he *wanted* was not to be nailed down into the things *you* thought he should do. He didn't need your permission to be who he was."

"Perhaps not," Rihad said, and he heard a note he didn't quite recognize in his own voice. Profound sadness, perhaps, that he doubted would ever leave him now. It cracked in him like temper. "But perhaps he could have used my support."

Her lips parted then, her expression confused, as if he'd spoken that last part in Arabic.

"Your support?" she echoed. "What do you mean?"

Rihad was furious. And something that felt a great deal like lost, besides. He had always known precisely what he had to do and how to do it. He had always known his path and how to walk it. He didn't know this. He didn't know how to navigate it—because it was too late.

Omar was dead, and Rihad had loved him—yet never truly known him.

The grief he'd understood would always be with him seemed to triple inside of him with every passing moment. Became darker. Thicker. And woven in with it was guilt. That he hadn't seen. That he hadn't looked. That he'd accepted his own brother at face value, even when doing so had meant thinking the worst of him.

He hated this. He hated himself. He hated all those wasted years.

"None of this explains you," Rihad bit out at Sterling, because she was there. Because she'd participated in this deception. Because she'd known his brother in a way he never would, and he was small enough to resent that, just then. "If he wanted a beard, why did he not marry years ago and cement it? And if he was going to be in a fake relationship with a woman, why did he not choose a woman who would raise no objections? Why you?"

"That seems to be the sticking point," she pointed out, her lovely eyes flashing with something heavier than temper. Darker. He felt another stab of guilt, and hated that, too. "Not so much why he did it, but that he did it with a woman like me."

"Because it's impractical." He wanted to punch something. He wanted to rage. He settled for seething at her instead. "You are a lightning rod of controversy. Why not choose a woman who would have flown beneath the radar?"

"Why don't we conduct a séance?" Sterling suggested in that same sarcastic tone, her pretty eyes narrow and dark on his. "You can lecture him just like this. I'm sure it will have the same effect now as it clearly did when he was still alive."

He didn't know when he'd drifted closer to her, as if she was some kind of magnet. Only that they were much too close then, and he wanted to touch her too much, and that was only one of the reasons he was furious.

It was the easiest reason.

"Don't." Sterling's eyes were glittering yet her mouth was vulnerable and Rihad wanted her. God, how he wanted her.

"Don't what?" he asked. "You were never my brother's lover."

"That doesn't mean I have any desire to be yours."

Yet he could see the faint tremor beneath her skin. He could see the flush across her cheeks. He knew her desire as well as he knew his own.

"Liar." But he said it as if it was very nearly a compliment.

She didn't contradict him, and the world was still so far away. There was only her. Here. And there had already been too many lies. There had been too much hidden and for too long, and Omar was lost.

His brother had never trusted him. Neither did Sterling. And he couldn't have said why he felt both so keenly. So harshly. As if they were the same thing. As if he could no longer trust himself.

"Help me solve the puzzle you present," he urged her in a rough whisper. "Why did he have a child with you? What did he hope to gain?"

She looked confused and slightly bereft. "He imagined that if he had a child, that would show you that he wasn't as irresponsible as you thought he was, even without you knowing the truth."

"That is a fine sentiment, Sterling, but all the reasons I married you held true for him, too."

"I doubt very much it was his intention to die," she threw back at him. "If he hadn't, maybe we would have married. Had he told me the reasons why that would help Leyla, I would have relented. But we'll never know what might have happened, will we?"

"I know that if he'd come to me, if he'd told me, I would not have turned my back on him. That's what I know." Rihad let out a long breath. "I will never understand why he did not."

Sterling made a frustrated noise. "That might have a bit more weight if you hadn't spent all these years acting as if he was a communicable disease."

He made a sound of protest, but she wasn't listening to him. Instead, she thrust one of her fists at him as if she wanted to hit him, but held herself back at the last moment.

"All you did was talk about how you had to clean up after him, as if he was garbage." And her voice was so bitter then. Her blue eyes the darkest he'd ever seen them. "Maybe if he'd thought he could trust you, if you cared about anything besides the damned country, he might have risked coming out to you."

"I loved him."

Again that fist, not quite making contact with his chest.

"Actions speak louder than words, Rihad. Don't blame Omar for your failure to treat him like a person. That's on you. That's *entirely* on you."

And whatever was left inside of him shattered at that.

Leaving him nothing but a howling emptiness, and the uncomfortable ring of a truth within it that he'd have given anything not to face.

"Damn you," he whispered, his tone harsh and broken, and he didn't try to hide it.

Then he reached for her, because he knew, somehow, that Sterling was the only person alive who could soothe that shattered thing in him—

But she flinched away from him and threw up her arms, as if she'd expected him to haul off and hit her.

As if, he understood as everything inside of him screeched to a halt and then turned cold, someone had done so before.

CHAPTER EIGHT

STERLING FLINCHED, WHEN she knew better than that. But she couldn't seem to help herself.

She'd finally pushed him too far. She'd felt safe with him all this time, safer than she'd ever felt with another man, but that was before. She'd gone over the edge at last and she'd seen that broken look on his face.

She knew what it meant. She remembered too well.

She expected the hit. It had been a long, long time, but she thought she could take it. There was no warding off a blow from a man as strong as he was or as close, but if she could take the inevitable fall well, it wouldn't immobilize her. The trick was not to tense up too much in anticipation, and then to curl into a tight ball against the kick—

"Sterling," Rihad said then, in that low, dark way of his that rippled through her, making her want to cry. Making her want him, too, which she thought was evidence that she was deeply sick in the head. Twisted all the way through, the way they'd always told her she was. "What do you think is happening here?"

"Please," she whispered, trying to stand tall, to square her shoulders despite the fact she couldn't stop shaking. "Just don't wake the baby. I don't want her to see."

And she closed her eyes, tried not to brace herself too much and waited for him to hit her.

The way her foster parents always had.

She heard nothing. For one lifetime, then another.

Then, finally, Rihad's voice, but he wasn't speaking to her. He spoke in Arabic, and she didn't have to understand the words he used to know he was issuing orders again in that matter-of-fact, deeply autocratic way of his that was as much a part of him as breathing.

Then again, the quiet.

The breeze above and the water all around, and she kept her eyes shut tight because the quiet was the trick. It was always a trick. The false sense of security had always, always tripped her up. The moment she'd thought it wasn't going to happen and looked to see was the moment they'd laid her flat.

She heard footsteps, then the sound of Leyla's buggy being wheeled away, and her stomach turned over, then plummeted. He was sending the baby off with the nurses, as she'd asked. That meant—

She flinched away from his hand on her arm, making it that much worse. Her eyes flew open and met his, burning dark, dark gold and far too close, and she nearly bit off her tongue.

"I'm sorry," she whispered hurriedly, in a panic she couldn't control, even when he let go of her and stepped back. "I didn't mean to flinch."

He studied her for a long, long time.

"Sterling," he said, very quietly, but somehow with more power behind it than she'd ever heard him use before. "Who hit you?"

And everything inside of Sterling ground to a lurching, nauseating halt. She couldn't risk this. She should never have flinched. Open up that old can of worms and he would *see*. He would *know*.

She didn't think it through, she simply catapulted herself across the wedge of space between them, trusting he would catch her. She didn't ask herself how she knew he would.

But he did.

His arms came around her as her chest collided with his, and all of that panic and all of those old ghosts shimmered into something else entirely.

His seductive heat poured through her. Into her. Chasing away all those old cobwebs she couldn't afford to let him see. *He couldn't know.*

She didn't want to think too much about *why* that was the worst thing she could imagine. The very worst. She only knew, without a shred of doubt, that it was.

"Exactly what do you think you are doing?" he asked, but his voice was as gentle as his hands against her.

And yet she could feel how hot he was, hot and hard and deliciously male against her, everywhere. He wanted her. It was a revelation. He was so hot that she might have thought he was feverish, had she not been looking straight up into those dark gold eyes of his, where she could see he wasn't the least bit unwell.

Dark and beautiful and much too close to all the parts of her she didn't want him to see, perhaps. But not sick.

Sterling was more than a little bit worried that she was the sick one here, but she shoved that thought aside. There was no time left to worry about any of that. About the strange revelations this morning had wrought, much less what they meant or the repercussions they might have. She couldn't let her mind spin out that way. She couldn't see the future, so there was no use panicking about it.

She could only do her best to confuse the present in the easiest and most direct way available to her before Rihad talked them both to the point of no return. Before he saw who she really was and was as disgusted as everyone else had always been.

So that was what she did.

Sterling pressed against him in what she hoped was an excellent show of wanton abandonment, winding her arms around the strong column of his neck, her mouth actually watering as she let her gaze move from that smooth, brown sweep of skin to his marvelous mouth that was now *right there*—

"Sterling," Rihad said repressively, but his hands were flush against her hips and he wasn't pushing her away. And she could feel him against her belly, so hard where she was so soft and yielding. The wild sensation made her shudder all the way through and then arch against him.

As if this wasn't the man she'd tried to run from, so long ago in New York, so sure he would ruin her.

As if this wasn't the man she'd thought was about to haul off and hit her moments before.

Or maybe because it was him. Because she'd snapped into a very old, horribly familiar place and he hadn't hit her after all. He'd looked appalled at the very idea.

And he wanted her. Even with that glimpse of the truth about her, he wanted her.

He wasn't like any other man she'd ever known. And that shattering thing swirled inside her, making her feel something rather more like truly wanton after all. That maddening heat, storming through her limbs and gathering low in her belly, making her feel hot and ripe and *hungry*—

She arched into him, harder this time, then went up on her toes and kissed him.

And everything exploded.

His mouth was divine torture, his kiss insane. Rihad took control almost the second it began, one of his hands moving to wrap itself in her hair, the better to hold her head where he wanted it, the other a hard, wild encouragement at her hip.

He angled his head for a better fit, and then he simply…*took*.

And she loved it.

Rihad kissed like a starving man, as if Sterling wasn't the only one scraped raw and left aching by this hungry thing between them. He kissed as if there was nothing at all for her to do but go along for the ride, wherever he took them. He kissed her until she was shivering against him in uncontrollable reaction, need and longing and the rich headiness of desire making her dizzy. And still so needy it hurt.

She couldn't get close enough. She couldn't taste him deeply enough. She didn't care if she could breathe, if her feet touched the ground, and when he shifted to haul her against him and then lifted her high in the air, the only thing she could think to do was kiss him again.

Harder. Deeper. Longer. Hotter.

He wrapped her legs around his waist and held her there, twined around him with no other support, making her tremble at the strength he displayed so offhandedly— and then he shifted again, so their hips dragged against each other, his hardness against the part of her that was the neediest, and she moaned into his mouth.

She'd never liked being touched. But she found that didn't apply to Rihad, who couldn't seem to touch her *enough*.

And right at that moment, she didn't care why that was. She would die if he knew, she thought. If he comprehended how untouched she truly was.

It wasn't until her back came up against something that she realized it wasn't just that spinning in her head that was making her feel loose and adrift—he'd walked over and laid her out on the table like his very own banquet.

"Reach up," he ordered her, sounding more like a king than she'd ever heard him sound before, and there was probably something deeply wrong with her that she liked it. More than liked it—that hot, dark note in his voice swept over her skin as if he'd used his mouth against her, his mouth and his wicked tongue. "Hold on."

She did as he asked. As he *commanded*. She didn't even think twice about it, and not only because she wanted him to think she was that slut everyone believed she was, but also because that was so much easier than who she really was.

Sterling reached up over her head and grabbed the far edge of the table as he leaned in harder, pressing his hips against hers even as this new position made her back arch, as if she was offering up her breasts to him.

She was. She hoped she looked as if she'd done this a thousand times before—or even if she didn't, that he'd be too interested in her breasts to care.

He smiled dangerously as he looked down at the place their bodies pressed together, and Sterling felt the glow of that sweep over her. Through her, hard and

hot and needy, until it settled like a lightning bolt between her legs.

She bucked against him, helpless against these new
sensations, and he laughed.

And then he bent down and found her nipple through
the gauzy material of her dress with that dangerously
clever mouth of his, so hot and so demanding, and
sucked it straight into all that heat.

Sterling lost her mind.

There was nothing then, but the fire that rolled
through her, one bright flame after the next, building
toward something so immense, so impossible, that she
would have been afraid of it if she'd been able to catch
her breath.

But Rihad didn't allow that.

He pressed the proof of his need hard into the place
she hungered for him the most, soft and wet and wild
for him even through the trousers he wore, with her
ankles locked in the small of his strong back. He set
a lazy, mind-melting rhythm, and Sterling could do
nothing but meet it, shuddering more with every roll
of his lethal hips.

She didn't know what she was doing. But she couldn't
seem to stop.

His mouth teased her breasts through her dress while
his hands streaked beneath it, testing her shape, her
heat. Learning all kinds of things about her. That she
rarely bothered with a bra, even these days when her
breasts were still bigger than they'd been before her
pregnancy. That a careful pinch against one nipple and
a deep tug on the other made her clutch her legs tighter

around him and ride him shamelessly, rubbing herself against him as wantonly as she could—

And then it slammed into her.

Like a train.

She cried out, but he was there, licking the sound of it from her lips, moving his own hips harder against hers, making it go on and on and on.

Making her shatter, then shatter again, then shatter once more.

Changing everything.

Changing the whole world.

Turning Sterling into someone new.

And when it was over, he let her drop her legs from around his waist and took a step back while she simply lay sprawled there on the table in a thousand pieces, trying to breathe.

It took a while and even then, it was a shaky thing.

When she sat up and pulled her dress back down to cover her, Rihad stood there above her, his dark face hard and his golden eyes glittering. He folded his arms over his powerful chest and considered her for a long, breathless moment, as if he wasn't still so aroused that she could see the proof of it pressing against the front of his trousers, hard and thick, and how could she still want him? Even now?

Even as the events of this morning flooded her, making her question a lot of things. Her sanity chief among them.

"Congratulations, Sterling," Rihad said in that low, rough voice of his that kicked up that fire in her all over again. "You succeeded in distracting me. How long do you think that will work?"

* * *

It had worked all too well, Rihad thought a few days later, as he sat in his luxuriously appointed offices and found it impossible to concentrate on matters of state.

Because she haunted him.

Her taste. The sounds she'd made as she'd writhed beneath him. The scent of her skin. The sweet perfection of her touch.

He found he couldn't think of much else. Especially during the meals they took together in his garden, where they both acted as if that scene *right there on the table* hadn't happened. They outdid each other with crisp politeness.

But it hummed beneath everything. Every clink of silver against fine china. Every sip of wine. Every glance that caught and held. Every movement they each made.

It was a madness in his blood, infecting him.

Or she was.

Because Rihad hardly knew himself these days. His entire relationship with his brother had been a lie. He was hung up on a woman he'd married while he'd believed she was Omar's mistress—and he had lusted after her while believing it. He was more enamored by the day with a tiny child who was not his in fact, but who felt like his in practice. He felt as if he was reeling through his life suddenly, unmoored and uncertain, and he had no idea how to handle such an alien sensation.

It was as if there was nothing left to hold on to. Or, more to the point, as if the only thing he wanted to hold on to was Sterling—as if he was as bewitched by her as he'd always thought his brother had been.

Maybe his enemies were not wrong to threaten invasion. Rihad was beginning to think it would be a kindness.

He was halfway through yet another inappropriate daydream about his wife when his personal mobile rang with a familiar ringtone.

Rihad dismissed his ministers with a regal wave and then swiped to open the video chat.

His sister gazed back at him from the screen, looking as defiant as ever.

"Amaya." He kept his voice calm, though it was harder than it should have been, and he didn't want to think about why that was, all of a sudden, or who was to blame for his endless lack of control. "Have you called to issue your usual taunts?"

"The quick brown fox always jumps over the lazy dog, Rihad." Her dark eyes were a shade lighter than the fall of thick dark hair she'd pulled forward over one shoulder, and it irritated him that she was both unquestionably beautiful and entirely too much like her treacherous mother. Smarter than was at all helpful and not in the least bit loyal to the Bakrian throne. It made her unpredictable and he'd always hated that—at least, he'd always thought he had. "I'm only giving you a much-needed demonstration."

"I feel adequately schooled."

"Obviously not. I can see you scanning behind me for details on my location. Don't bother. There aren't any that will help you find me." The light of battle lit her face, and he stopped trying to find any sort of geographic marker in what looked like a broom closet around her. "Are you ready to call off this marriage? Set me free?"

This was where Rihad normally outlined her responsibilities, reminded her that despite what she might have preferred, she was a Bakrian princess and she had a duty to her country. That it didn't matter how many years she'd spent knocking around various artistic, bohemian communities with her mother pretending she was nothing more than another rootless flower child, she couldn't alter the essential truth of her existence. That her university years in Montreal might have given her the impression that her life was one of limitless choices in all directions, but that was not true, not for her, and the sooner she accepted that the happier she would be.

He'd been telling her all of this for months. Years.

None of those conversations had been at all successful.

Today, he thought of the brother he'd treated as if he was a failure, the brother he'd claimed he'd loved when he'd never given him the opportunity to be himself. Not in Rihad's presence anyway. He thought of the way Sterling, the only woman—hell, the only *person*—who had ever defied him to his face with such a lack of fear, had flinched as if she expected him to beat her, all because she'd told him the truth.

He thought that perhaps he had no business being a king, if he was such a remarkably bad one.

"I wish I could do that, Amaya," he said after a long moment. "More than you know."

She stared at him as if she couldn't believe he'd said that. He wasn't sure he could, either.

He shrugged. "These are precarious times. The only possible way we will maintain our sovereignty is to unite with Daar Talaas. But you know this."

"There must be another way."

"If there was, don't you think I would have found it?" He sat back in his chair, his eyes on the screen and on his sister. "It does not give me any particular pleasure to insist you do something you are so opposed to that you've been on the run all this time."

"But…?" she prompted, though he noticed that defiant way she held herself had softened.

"But Kavian is a man who follows the ancient ways, and there is only one kind of alliance he holds sacred. Blood." He studied Amaya then, saw the expression that moved over her face, that hint of something like heat in her gaze. "And I think you know this all too well, don't you? Because while you were not exactly thrilled at the idea, you didn't run away until after you met him at your engagement reception. Did he do something to you?"

Alliance or not, Rihad would kill him. But Amaya only flushed then, though she tried to cover it with a frown.

"The reality of the situation merely impressed itself upon me, that's all. I realized that I'm not a Stone Age kind of a girl."

He didn't believe her, but that was hardly his business.

"I sympathize," he said instead, and the thing of it was, he did. He truly did.

"And I'm skeptical."

"Amaya, no one knows more about marrying for the sake of the kingdom than I do. I'm on my second such marriage."

"That doesn't exactly recommend the ordeal." Amaya's frown deepened. Her eyes searched his for perhaps a moment too long. "You're not the happiest man I've ever met."

And yet in comparison to Kavian, the desert warrior

renowned for his ability to wage war like an ancient warlord, Rihad was a nonstop comedy show. Neither one of them pointed that out and yet it hung there between them anyway.

For a moment they only gazed at each other, separated by their years, the screen, her continued refusal to surrender to the inevitable.

"Don't believe everything you read," he advised her. "My marriage is not an ordeal." He felt a sharp pang of disloyalty then, because he'd forgotten about Tasnim entirely. It was as if he really was a stranger, inhabiting the same body but utterly changed, all because of one lush woman and her artlessly addictive mouth. "And my first marriage might not have been a love match, but it was good. We were content."

Amaya's hand crept up to her neck and she cupped her hand there, then looked away.

"Kavian is not the kind of man who is ever going to be *content*," she said, so softly he almost didn't hear her. The old version of himself would have pretended he hadn't.

"I wish I could call it off," he told her quietly, and saw her swallow hard. Was he that harsh? That she had no idea that he wanted to protect her—that he would have if he could? "But you signed all the papers. You made your initial vows. By the laws of Daar Talaas, you are already his."

She shuddered, and when she looked at him again, he felt that great loosening inside him again, as if he'd lost this, too. This relationship with the only sibling he had left. This sister who clearly had no idea that he loved her, too.

He felt an unknown and unpleasant sensation swamp

him then and realized he'd felt it before. When Sterling had stood there before him with her eyes closed and her head bowed, visibly forcing herself to relax, the better to take a hit he hadn't been planning to deliver.

Helplessness.

He loathed it.

"Amaya." Her head jerked around and her eyes met his, and he saw confusion there. And something else, something a little more like haunted. "You are not a mere pawn. I care what happens to you. But I can't fix this."

"So I am doomed." And her voice cracked on that last word. "There is no hope."

"You can appeal to Kavian himself—"

"I'd have better luck appealing to a sandstorm in the desert!"

"Amaya." But he didn't know what to say. He was a goddamned king and what was the point? He couldn't save anyone. "I'm sorry."

"So am I." She shook her head, as if she was shaking something off. "I don't want war, Rihad. I don't want Bakri to fall. But I don't want to be Kavian's... *possession*, either. I won't."

And her screen went dark.

Leaving Rihad alone with his thoughts and his regrets, which were darker still.

CHAPTER NINE

THE SOUND OF the helicopter's rotor blades faded off into the distance, taking with it Sterling's halfhearted hopes that they might be called back to the palace to tend to some kind of governmental issue that simply couldn't wait.

And then the only sound—in and around and between the brightly colored tents tucked there between the towering desert sand dunes and arrayed around the series of tree-lined pools that shouldn't have existed in so arid a place at all—was the wind. It danced over the tops of the tents, making the hard canvas bend and stretch beneath the high sun far above, and then clattered its way through the palm trees.

Sterling was glad, because otherwise she was certain the only noise around for the miles and miles of uninhabited Bakrian desert they'd covered to get here would be the crazy pounding of her heart.

Rihad, of course, didn't appear to hear any of it. He was conducting a conversation in rapid-fire Arabic into the satellite phone at his ear, striding toward one of the larger tents nearer the water as if he expected her to follow along obediently in his wake.

Instead, Sterling stayed where she was. She tilted her

head back and let the desert sun play over her face. She liked the lick of heat, the tease of the dry wind against her skin and in the ends of the hair she'd scraped into a low ponytail beneath a wide-brimmed hat. She liked the murmur of the water from the nearby pools, the suggestion of cool, inviting shade beneath the trees and inside the tents. She would have been enchanted by the whole *desert oasis* thing altogether were it not for the fact he'd insisted she leave Leyla behind with the nurses, which was making her anxious.

And for what she suspected Rihad meant to accomplish here, which made her…something a lot more complicated than simply *anxious*.

"Maybe we can go in a month or two," she'd said when he'd brought up their perception-altering honeymoon again at another one of their dinners. This one had been more intimate, set up in his private dining suite with the wraparound balcony that opened up over the whole of Bakri City, where all she could seem to think about was his hands on her body, his hardness clenched tight between her legs. "When Leyla is a little bigger and will be better about me going away for a night."

Rihad had appeared focused on the food on his plate that night, not on her, though she should have known better than to believe that.

"It was not an invitation, as I think you know," he'd said after a moment. "It was an order. A royal command, even."

"Apparently, I have to remind you yet again that I'm not yours to command."

He'd laughed, and she'd started in her chair, because it had been genuine. The sound of it had cascaded over her, as if it was poured straight from the sun. "Do you think so?"

She tried to sound prim. Not at all like the sort of woman who would climax all over a man on a wrought-iron table one summer morning. "I'm not one of your subjects, Rihad."

"You are my queen." His gaze had risen to meet hers then and she'd flushed hot and red. His dark gold eyes had been alive with something like merriment, and there'd been hints of that laughter in his voice when he'd continued. "And in the spirit of transparency between us, which I know is your dearest hope—"

"What's wrong with murky?" she'd protested, aware she'd sounded as cranky as she had desperate. "I like a good swamp, especially in my marriage."

His eyes had gleamed, laughter and light, and she'd felt undone.

He would unravel her completely. She had no doubt.

He'd already started.

"It will be more than a single night in the desert. I already told you it would be two weeks. And so it will." When she'd started to argue he'd only smiled. "I'd resign yourself to the inevitable, Sterling. Have I yet to promise you anything that didn't happen exactly as I said it would?"

She hadn't been able to breathe. But that hadn't stopped her mouth from moving.

"Are you going to command me to have sex with you, too?" she'd asked in that same absurdly overpolite tone, as if she was inquiring after high tea. "Consummation on demand?"

And she'd had no words to describe what his smile had done to her then, or how that lazy, predatory gleam in his dark gold eyes had made her feel. God, the way it had made her *feel*. How it had sneaked through her, tangling all around and making her hollow and needy, scared and yearning at once.

Did she *want* him to command her? *Reach up,* he'd ordered her that morning. *Hold on.* Was that why she'd asked?

"If you insist," he'd said after a moment, in a dark-edged way that had made everything inside of her feel the way he'd sounded. Like honey, sweet and slow. She remembered shattering all around him, again and again. She shivered just remembering it. "Is that how you like it, Sterling? Do you prefer to give orders on the street and take them in bed?"

It was as if he'd read her mind, and she'd told herself stoutly that she hated that. And that he hadn't, of course.

She'd sniffed as if she found this discussion crass beyond measure. "Not from you."

Rihad had only smiled again, harder and edgier than before, and it had banged through Sterling like a symphony of gongs. "We'll see. We leave in two days' time. I suggest you resign yourself to the torture."

And now she was far, far away from anything even resembling civilization. The helicopter ride had taken at least two hours and they'd left the city limits within the first twenty minutes. There was nothing for miles in any direction. There was nothing here except forced intimacy and, she thought while her stomach cartwheeled around inside of her, nothing at all to keep her from exploring the one man alive whose touch she didn't seem to mind.

"I've dismissed all but the most essential staff." His voice made her jump and she opened her eyes to find him propped up against the nearest palm tree, his dark gold gaze simmering as it touched hers. "There is no one else here but the two of us and, farther out, my security guards to keep watch over the perimeter."

"You mean, to keep me from running away from you."

He smiled again, and that other night at the palace hadn't been a fluke. It was devastating. It was almost as powerful as his kiss. It made her feel that same mix of weakness and wonder, and she didn't have the slightest idea what to do about it.

"I mean, my most faithful and devoted guards are there to protect you whether you like it or not." He'd let out a quiet sort of laugh. "But yes. Part of that protection would include returning you to my tender embrace should you wander too far from the oasis. The desert sands can be so treacherous."

"How thoughtful." But her mouth was pulling at the corners, as if her smile wanted to break free despite her own wishes. "Will you have men to guard the pools as well, in case I am tempted to drown myself rather than suffer your company?"

His laugh was deeper then. Richer. It was like drowning, indeed, in a masculine version of the best chocolate she could imagine, decadent and addictive.

She was in so much trouble.

"It depends which pool you mean to drown yourself in," he said, as if he was giving the issue due consideration. "This nearest one will take some work. It's barely knee-deep. You're more likely to drown in your wineglass."

"That can be arranged."

He moved closer. He should have looked like any

other man, the epitome of casual in nothing but a white oxford shirt and sand-colored trousers, but this was Rihad. He *was* the king. It didn't seem to matter what he wore; nothing could conceal that low-edged hum of power he carried with him wherever he went.

"Shall we discuss our agenda, now that we're here?" he asked when he was much too close. When she couldn't seem to do anything but lose herself somewhere between that look on his face and the pounding of her heart.

"Our honeymoon has an agenda?" She fought to keep her voice light and airy—and to keep from leaping away from him because she knew, somehow, that he would know full well she wanted to do the opposite. "Royal sheikhs in their luxurious oasis retreats really *aren't* like us."

"Consider this nothing more than a statement of intent, Sterling."

She wanted to throw something back at him, to make this interchange all about amusing banter and not about the rest of the things that circled all around them, pressing in on them, as flattening and searingly hot as the desert sun high over their heads.

"And what exactly do you intend?" she asked, but her throat was so dry, and he was so close. He stood there, much too near to her, so that she imagined she could feel the heat of him. So that her palms itched to touch him again—and that unnerved her more than anything else.

"I think you know what I want you to tell me," he said quietly.

She didn't want to meet his gaze then, but she did. And it shuddered all the way through her in a way that made her feel raw and vulnerable. But not afraid. Something else that she wasn't certain she understood.

"No," she said.

And she didn't know what that meant, even as she said it. No, she didn't know what he meant? No, she wasn't going to tell him? No, in general?

But he smiled as if she'd whispered him a line or two of poetry and reached over to skate the backs of his fingers down the side of her face. *Undoing her,* she thought. He was tearing her down, pulling her apart, right where they stood.

"And I think you know the rest of what I want," he said in a low voice.

"I know this will be hard for you to understand," she said, trying to sound strong. Tough. Worldly and amused, in that way she'd perfected years ago. "But not everyone gets what they want all the time. Some people never get what they want at all. It's a fact of life when you're not literally the king of all you survey."

Rihad smiled, and the heat where his fingers caressed her cheek blossomed deep within her.

"But I am."

And still he smiled when all she could do was stare up at him, mute and undone and all those other things that tangled up inside of her and made her this shockingly susceptible to him.

Then he dropped his hand and stepped back, and Sterling felt that like a loss. She pulled in a breath, amazed she was still standing on her own two feet. Truly astonished she hadn't simply keeled over from all that intensity.

"I have some things I must attend to," he told her. "The sad truth is that the leader of a country is never truly on holiday, despite what he might wish. But you will join me for dinner. In the meantime, Ushala will lead you to your tent and see that you are settled in."

"What if I don't want to join you for dinner?" she asked.

She thought they both knew that she wasn't really talking about dinner.

And in any case, Rihad only smiled.

Sterling disappeared into one of the sleeping tents that functioned as a luxurious guest room out here in his family's private oasis. Rihad took a few calls as the afternoon wore on, impatient with this life of his that could not allow him anything resembling a real holiday. Not even a honeymoon.

He opted not to think too much about the fact that when he'd gone on a honeymoon previously, he'd welcomed the opportunity to work from the oasis, and neither he nor Tasnim had expected to see much of each other outside of their carefully polite meals.

But then, Sterling was different. Perhaps he'd known that from the first moment he'd seen her, so long ago now on that Manhattan sidewalk.

She did not emerge again until the sun dipped low and began to paint the dunes in the shifting colors of sunset. Reds and oranges, pinks and golds, and Sterling walking toward him in the middle of it all like another work of art.

Rihad sat in one of the *majlis*, a seating area marked off with a soft rug beneath him, bright pillows all around in the Bedouin style and a low table stretched out beneath a graceful canopy. It opened on the sides to let the evening in as he sipped a cool drink and watched

the sunset outdo itself before him, as if for his pleasure alone.

After a glance to make sure she was coming to
him—of her own free will, which pleased him, though
he imagined he'd have sought her out if she hadn't and
he wasn't certain what that told him about himself—
Rihad didn't look up as Sterling approached him, didn't
take his eyes off the horizon.

Almost as if he worried that if he did, his best inten-
tions would simply crumble into sand and blow away.

He smiled at the glorious spectacle laid out before
him instead, the colors changing and blooming as he
watched. He never tired of the desert. How could he—
how could anyone? The landscape was constantly shifting, yet always the same. The great bowl of the sky
stretched high above with these magical, daily displays
of fierce natural splendor. It reminded him who he was.
It reminded him that Bakri was as much a part of him
as he was of it. Just as the sky and the land were fused
into this stunning unity twice a day as the sun rose
and fell, so, too, was his family a part of this country.
Twined together, made one.

That was what a marriage was, at its best. What it
was *supposed* to be.

What he was determined this one would be, no matter what he had to do to get there.

Rihad did not choose to analyze all the reasons why
his need for this burned in him. He only knew that it
did.

She settled herself down across from him at the low
table with that innate grace of hers that was beginning
to feel something like addictive.

"Does your tent suit?" he asked her, as if they were

meeting at some or other royal exercise, where the highest protocols were observed.

"It's lovely," she replied in the same tone.

Rihad bit back a smile and waved to the servants. They appeared at once, filling the low table between them with various dishes, from perfectly grilled skewers of lamb to a pile of handmade flatbread, a generous pot of homemade hummus, assorted other dipping sauces and side dishes. Rihad took the opportunity to study this woman, this *wife* of his. She was nothing like Tasnim. He couldn't remember a single moment with his first wife that had ever felt like this—this seething thing, nearly at a boil, that thrummed along beneath his skin and made him feel predatory and possessive even when she wasn't in front of him.

And much, much more so when she was.

She wore another one of her dresses and a flowing pashmina she wrapped tightly around her like a blanket. More to continue to conceal herself from him as much as possible, he thought with no little amusement, than to ward off the night air. Her lustrous strawberry blond hair was pulled back into what was, for her, a merely serviceable ponytail at her nape, but then, elegance was stamped into her bones. She couldn't help but appear chic, even when she was attempting to look dowdy. She'd been haunting in those teenaged photographs that had taken the modeling world by surprise years back, all high cheekbones, world-weary blue eyes and that hooker's mouth of hers. More than a decade later, she was objectively, inarguably stunning, no matter what lengths she went to hide it.

And Rihad was merely a man.

He lounged there against his pillows and watched her eat her dinner with evident relish, this woman who could knock men flat like dominoes. Take down whole kingdoms. Wreck worlds.

Or maybe that was just what she'd done to him, when he'd been expecting something so much different.

"You're staring at me as if I'm an animal in a zoo," she pointed out crisply when she'd demolished a few lamb chops and several heaping spoonfuls of the grain and greens salads. "It's going to give me indigestion."

"I'm waiting for you to finish eating," he said lazily. "You're building up your energy, are you not? For the sex. Consummation on command, I believe you called it. A warning, Sterling. I'm very demanding."

"The sex," she repeated slowly. There wasn't a flicker of reaction on her perfect face, or even in those sky-blue eyes of hers when she fixed them on him, but he knew better. He could feel the air itself sizzle between them. "Am I to understand that you'll be performing a solo act? Right here, out in the open? How fascinating. You'll understand if I don't watch, I hope. I wouldn't want my stomach to turn at a delicate moment and throw you off your stroke."

He only watched her as the servants cleared all the plates between them and then piled the table high again with an array of tempting desserts—but Sterling was looking at him with that fire in her gaze and he couldn't have imagined any better treat than her.

"You're sitting here in silence, Sterling," he pointed out, playing up the languid desert king because he could see the way it got to her. He could see the way she shifted against her pillows, as if she couldn't quite get comfortable. "I assumed that you'd decided we should jump right into the sex rather than have a frank discussion." He smiled. "I'm perfectly all right with that, if it's what you wish."

She most certainly did not wish, Sterling told herself then. But she had the growing notion that she was lying to herself.

And worse, that he knew it.

"Do you ever have interactions with anyone in which you aren't threatening them?" she asked, mildly enough. "Whether directly or indirectly?"

"Most of my interactions are political in nature," he replied, a vision of male ease as he lounged there and watched her too closely, his dark eyes glittering in the light thrown by too many hanging lanterns to count. "So, no. I don't have any conversations that do not involve jockeying for power, or position, or status, or economic gain."

"You are aware that some people have conversations that involve none of those things?"

A faint crook to that perfect mouth. "I've heard rumors."

"I will have to decline your lovely offer," she said, and smiled at him in the polite-yet-distant way she'd perfected in New York. "I've never been to an oasis before and I think I'd like to take a swim in the middle of a desert. Your marvelous suggestion that we delve into my past and/or me, personally, while tempting, will have to wait."

She thought he would throw something back at her, but he only continued to study her with that small smile in the corner of his mouth. Sterling took that as acquiescence—or whatever it was when powerful men gave in, without seeming to give at all.

Sterling rose and walked past him toward the deepest of the three pools that shimmered there only a few steps from where they'd had their dinner. All the pools were hung with their own lanterns, each casting a dancing, mellow light over the dark waters. It made the water seem something more than simply inviting. Mysterious. Seductive. She stepped onto the mat that had been laid out there beneath the lightly rustling palm trees and kicked off her slides, then dropped her pashmina.

"You realize you are not fooling me, I hope," Rihad said almost conversationally, still lounging there beneath the canopy behind her. "I know exactly what you are doing."

"Swimming?" she asked over her shoulder. "You are correct, Your Royal Majesty. Your powers of observation are truly magnificent."

Then she pulled the floor-length, flowing dress she wore up and over her head, leaving herself in nothing at all but a very tiny, very provocative string bikini in a metallic, shiny gold.

She could feel his sudden stillness from behind her, predatory and vast, like an epic, nuclear implosion of the same hunger she knew beat in her, but she didn't turn back toward him. She didn't need to. *This* was the point. The tease. The distraction.

Getting him back a little bit. Making him pay.

And she'd spent enough time as a model to have rendered her nothing but practical, more or less, about her body. She might have given birth only a few months back. She might have a different shape now, and new marks like claws on a belly she doubted would ever be

concave again. But she was well aware of the power of
her curves. And she knew that standing there in a flirty
gold bikini would make it as hard for Rihad to sleep at
night as it had been for her since that morning in the
palace gardens.

Sterling was very good at this after all. She'd made a
living out of using her body like this, once upon a time.

But she didn't want to think about the past. She
wanted to keep it behind her, as long as she could. To-
night, she only wanted to make Rihad ache the way
that she ached.

She didn't look back at him, she looked at the inky
black surface of the pool, lit with dancing gold from the
lanterns, and it was like looking straight into Rihad's
mesmerizing gaze.

She dived right in.

CHAPTER TEN

THE WATER WAS COOL, CLEAR.

It was like a silken caress over her skin, long and luxurious at once, and if she could have, Sterling would have stayed beneath the surface of that pool forever. She let herself sink, then float beneath the surface, and pretended she could remain there. But eventually her lungs began to ache a little bit and she kicked back up into the night air.

To find Rihad much closer, squatting there at the edge of the water, his dark gaze fierce on hers. It made her heart leap inside her chest, so hard and so high she was surprised it didn't make the water ripple in reaction.

"Do you think you are safe in the water?" he asked her, and there were stark lines stamped on his face as he gazed at her. As if need was carving into him, the way she could feel it in her, too.

Whittling away at her until she didn't know what was left, or who she'd be when it was done.

"I think that safety is relative where you're concerned," she said now, perhaps a shade too flippantly. She was more enthusiastic about swimming than she was skilled at it, so she moved closer to the side of the pool, reaching out a hand to hold on to the edge. "Kings are not exactly known for putting the needs of their wives before their own."

"You know a great many kings, do you?"

She slicked her hair back, as aware of the way his dark gold eyes tracked the movement as if he'd used his own hands. And his attention was like a live wire, ferocious and total.

"I'm aware of the entire history of the planet, if that's what you mean."

Rihad studied her in that focused, too-incisive way of his that made her want to *do things* to escape it. Before he could see every last corner of her dirty little soul.

"I have a modest hope that I am less bloodthirsty than many of the kings who predate me," he was saying drily. "And I know I'm better to my wives than most of those, given I've yet to execute one."

"Was that on the table here?"

"We're talking about absolute power. It's all on the table. Something to remember the next time you're feeling feisty." But his mouth was crooked into that small smile of his she was beginning to find addictive, despite that steady gaze of his that made her tremble deep within. "But I can't imagine you really want to talk about the powers of the Bakrian monarchy, or the march of kings throughout time, do you?"

"I don't want to talk to you at all. I wanted to swim."

He indicated the pool behind her with a jerk of his fine chin. "Then by all means, Sterling. Swim."

But she didn't move.

They could have stayed frozen there for a decade. She'd never have known the difference. Only that she couldn't look away from him.

This man who had far more power than the others

she'd known, who'd taken theirs out on her because they'd considered her so beneath them. Rihad was autocratic. He certainly used his power. But never like that. Never so viciously.

Eventually, he reached down and traced a lazy, sensual pattern from one shoulder, across the very top of her chest, all the way to the other. Then back.

And she still didn't understand why his was the only touch that made her feel like this, wrapped up in a blaze of need and outside her own skin. She didn't understand why she wanted him, wanted more, *wanted*, when she'd never wanted any other man in her life.

When she'd never wanted any *touch* in her life.

She didn't understand any of this, only that when he touched her she wanted to sob out, and not because it hurt her. And when he didn't touch her, it was worse.

He'd made her into a woman she didn't understand at all. Maybe it was that she felt like a *woman* after all. Not a punching bag. Not a clothes hanger. Not an ornament. Not a mother. *A woman*, for the first time.

"I hate you," she whispered.

Just as she had at their wedding.

But this time, Rihad smiled, and it was as if that, too, burst into her and pried her wide-open however little she wanted to let him in.

"I am so sorry, little one," he murmured, his dark gold eyes on hers, and that look of his slid straight through her, too soft and too slick. It made her shake and this time, not only inside. "It's not so easy to make me the monster you wanted me to be, is it?"

"Maybe not," she whispered up at him, filled with that same wild urge to *do anything* to keep him from seeing the truth about her. Before it was too late. "But this is very easy, actually."

And Sterling reached up, grabbed hold of the arm he had propped on his knee as she braced her feet on the side of the pool, and she yanked him off balance.

Then she hauled the King of Bakri straight into the pool.

He sank like a stone, in a cascade of bubbles while a great wave slapped at her, and she was breathing so fast it hurt while the adrenaline—at her temerity, at the fact she'd actually done it—spiked inside of her. She'd made the split-second decision to get the hell out of that pool *right now* when he surfaced beside her, and Sterling realized that she was frozen in place. Paralyzed, more like.

Why on earth had she done that?

But Rihad laughed.

He tipped his beautiful face back and he laughed, hard and long, and she was tempted to think it was all a great big joke to him, to have her throw him fully dressed into a pool like that—but then he dropped his head back down, fixed that edgy gold gaze of his on her, and there wasn't a shred of laughter on his lethally beautiful face then.

"That, Sterling," he told her, his voice a sensual growl she felt in her sex as surely as if he was already touching her, "was a mistake."

And then he reached over, hooked a hard hand around her neck and yanked her to him.

He took her mouth as if he owned it, and Rihad thrilled to it—because he did. She was his. The sweep of her tongue against his. The way she yielded to him so quickly, so completely, meeting him and spurring him on.

This was *his* woman. *His* wife. *His*.

She wrapped her arms around his neck and held on, and he thought he might drown them both as he feasted on her, taking and taking, so hard and so good he thought he might die from it. He thought he might not care too much if he did.

There was no time left then. Not anymore. He had to be inside her, now, and nothing else mattered. Not her secrets. Not all the things she still hadn't told him and had gone to such lengths to avoid telling him. Nothing but this mad fire, this perfect kiss. The heft of her gorgeous breasts in their little scraps of gold, the slick glory of her taste.

His Sterling. His queen.

Somehow, he moved them to the shallower end of the pool, where he could stand. When he did, he trapped her between the pool's bank and his body. He felt the wind against the wet shirt on his back, but he didn't care. He only cared about Sterling. About this. Her hands digging into the flesh at his shoulders. Her legs moving to wrap around his hips again.

And for the first time in his entire adult life, Rihad stopped thinking.

He fumbled between them, wrestling with his soaked trousers to pull himself free. Then, his mouth still fused to hers, he reached down between them, out of finesse and out of his mind as he pushed her little bikini bottom to one side and stroked beneath it, straight into her soft, scalding heat.

"Rihad…" she moaned, straight into his mouth, and it was the sexiest thing he'd ever heard.

He didn't think. He moved his hand, he held her

close and then he simply thrust straight into her, hard and sure, making her truly his at last.

At last.

She made an odd sound, and he pulled back to look down at her lovely face, the haze clearing slightly.

Sterling's eyes were too big and hinted at some kind of emotion he didn't recognize. Rihad held himself still, and she breathed hard. Shakily. Once, then again.

"Are you all right, little one?" he asked quietly, still so deep inside of her he thought it might kill him. She was so hot, so wet. Snug around him, as if she'd been made to receive him exactly like this. "Did I hurt you? Are you not yet healed from giving birth?"

"No…" she said, as if she wasn't sure. Her blue gaze was dark, slick, in the light from the gently dancing lanterns overhead. He frowned as she continued. "I'm fine. I'm healed, I… It's just… It's weird, that's all."

"Weird," he repeated, as if the word didn't make sense, and slid back a few inches, experimentally, just to see what would happen—

And then, impossibly, Sterling McRae blushed.

Bright red. As if, Rihad thought in total fascination, she was entirely innocent. As if this was her first time.

But that was crazy.

Still, once the thought was there, Rihad couldn't seem to keep himself from indulging it. He'd wanted to lose himself in her, pound them both into delirious oblivion with all the pent-up need that had haunted his every thought of her for months now—but instead, he slowed down. He took his time.

He treated her like the virgin she couldn't possibly be.

He kissed her everywhere he could see that flushed

red skin, until the rosy glow she wore was for another reason entirely. He set a slow, lazy pace, easy and wicked at once, making sure that each time he slid away she clung to him a little more, then pulled him back to her a little harder. He used his mouth and his hands, his teeth and his voice, until she was writhing against him, mindless and moaning, just the way he'd wanted her.

Then he reached down, pressed hard against the center of her need and sent her flying.

And it was the most beautiful thing he'd ever seen. So damned beautiful it hurt—and he wasn't done.

When she came back to herself, panting and dazed, he went a little bit faster, a little bit harder. He held her where he wanted her and took her until that made her cry out, then splinter all over again, and that time, he went with her.

But he was in no doubt, even then.

Sterling was a virgin.

Or had been one anyway, before she'd entered this pool.

And now she was his.

Rihad was unusually quiet when he climbed from the pool and then pulled her out behind him, but Sterling was still floating off in the clouds somewhere, too lost in the sensations still storming through her body to care.

He lifted her up and swung her into his arms, then carried her over the sands to his tent, not seeming to notice that he was still in his soaking wet clothes. He shouldered his way inside, where Sterling blinked in the softly lit interior until her eyes adjusted. When they did, she had to bite back a gasp.

Because it was like walking into a dream. Where her

tent was like a desert rendition of a high-end hotel room, Rihad's was something else entirely. It was a pageant of scarlet and gold, from the wide bed on its magnificent, kingly platform to the seating areas, some with pillows on the floor arrayed around what looked like a fireplace, some with wide, inviting couches, some set carefully around what looked like a personal library. There were jeweled chests and thick rugs, tapestries and ornate screens to mark off separate areas, and it felt like all the half-formed fantasies Sterling had ever had about distant harems and the harshly beguiling men who ruled over them.

And he was far better than any fantasy she'd ever had, she knew now. Even the ones she'd had about him, little, though, she'd wanted to admit that to herself.

Rihad still didn't speak.

He stalked across the room and disappeared behind one of the screens, into what Sterling assumed was his own bathroom suite. She stood where she was, dripping onto the priceless carpet like a drowned thing, and when he returned, his face was set into an expression she couldn't begin to work out. And his gaze was so fierce she couldn't look at him directly—though that was not exactly a hardship, she thought, as her eyes dropped from his. He'd stripped off his wet clothes and was starkly, proudly naked, striding toward her as if it was the most natural thing in the world for him to do so.

She supposed it was. Even she understood that nudity was commonly a part of the whole sex thing.

The whole sex thing *that you've now done,* she reminded herself, still more than a little dazed by it. The act itself and the fact that she'd slipped across a kind of internal boundary line while she'd been shattering apart in Rihad's arms.

It was over. Virginity dispensed with quickly and efficiently, and the best part was, Rihad was none the wiser. No awkward conversations filled with explanations and confessions, no accusations of being a great big freak of nature—all the things she'd always feared would happen if she ever got around to this hadn't happened with Rihad.

And she was still so turned on, still so hungry for him, that she shook.

He picked her up again, as if she was as light as a doll—or as if she was utterly his, a thought that was so electrifying it burst inside of her like pain—and she should have protested that, but she didn't. This time, he set her down on the high, wide platform step next to the bed and set about peeling her bikini all the way from her body, his hands like hot brands where the wet material had chilled her skin.

He produced a towel from somewhere and dried her off, carefully and thoroughly, and before he was done she was restless and needy all over again, moving from foot to foot when he crouched down before her—

And he knew it, she realized, when he glanced up at her, his eyes glittering darkly and that lush mouth of his in a crooked curve.

Her breath left her in a rush.

Rihad wrapped his hands around her hips and lifted her, then tipped her back so she sprawled out on the high bed before him. Then he folded up her knees and held her there with those too-strong hands of his, all of her aching lower body open to him. He looked at her for a smoldering moment, then leaned down and licked his way deep into her heat.

Sterling made a sound that could only be described as a scream.

And he took his damned time, all over again. He tasted every contour, every fold. He took her femininity as relentlessly and totally as he'd taken her mouth, and she was burning up for him so quickly, so deliriously, that she had the wild thought that she might not survive it.

He laughed against the core of her and it went through her like lightning, and then once more, he threw her off the side of the planet into that sweet, hot oblivion.

This time, when she came back to him he'd crawled up over her on the bed. He lined up that hard, proud length with her most sensitive flesh and, when she gasped out his name, pushed in deep.

It was different this time. Darker, hotter.

Harder.

She felt the wave snap back, then swell, and she tossed her head against the bed, as afraid of what was coming as she was desperate for it.

"Beg me," he ordered her harshly against her ear as he held himself over her, and it was like its own caress, rough and wild.

And she didn't think. She didn't argue.

She obeyed. She begged.

And it made it that much better.

Hotter. Sweeter.

Rihad pistoned in and out of her, making her a creature she'd never imagined she could be. She tore at him. She scratched him. She pleaded with him and he laughed, and that made her plead all the more. She writhed and she held on, she met each hard thrust as if she'd been made for this. For him. As if she'd waited all this time, as if it hadn't been an accident, because she'd been meant for him all along.

She wanted it to last forever. She thought she might die if it did.

And this time, when she fell apart, he shouted out her name like a hoarse prayer and came with her.

She didn't know how long she slept, or if it was even sleep—maybe she'd simply passed out from the enormity of what had happened? What she'd finally done? But when she woke again, she was tucked up next to him and he was playing with her hair, sliding the slippery strands through those clever fingers of his, that enigmatic expression still on his darkly gorgeous face.

That face of his she felt was stamped inside her, somehow, like a brand.

Sterling felt made new. As if he'd taken her apart and put her back together, and she would never be quite the same. She felt deeply and irrevocably changed. Altered, as if she might not recognize herself in the mirror the next time she looked.

She felt as if he'd taught her how to fly.

And she couldn't tell him that. He couldn't know. It was a slippery slope—

"Sterling."

She jolted back to him, to that curious light in his eyes and that little curve to his deliciously full mouth.

"Rihad," she said, and she wondered if his name would always sound like that to her now. Like a poem.

"I want to ask you a question."

"Anything." She meant it. Especially if they could

keep doing this. Just a few hundred more times, she thought, and that might take the edge off.

He shifted closer to her, propped himself up on one elbow and smiled into her eyes.

"Tell me one thing," he said, in that voice of his, so low and now intimately connected to something deep inside of her, as if he could simply flip a switch and she would long for him. She did. His dark gold eyes gleamed. "How is it possible that you were a virgin?"

Sterling went very, very still. He reached over and pulled a long strand of her hair between his fingers again, and this time, he tugged. Gently enough, but it seared through her anyway.

"That's ridiculous," she said, though her voice sounded faint—or maybe she couldn't hear it very well, over the clatter of her heart against her ribs. Because what else could she say? "Who's ever heard of a virgin my age?"

His gaze held hers, steady and direct. "I didn't ask you whether or not you were a virgin, Sterling. I know you were." His lips curved into something tender if not quite a smile, and it pulled at her. "Hail Sterling, full of grace."

"It's true," she whispered, because the thought hadn't occurred to her, really. Not fully formed anyway. "I accidentally performed a virgin birth."

"I asked you how."

"The usual way." She blinked when his eyebrow arched. "By which I mean IVF, of course. I did tell you that your brother was gay."

"Yes, thank you." His voice was as dry as the desert all around them. "I gathered that, as I saw no heavenly host hanging about the pool just now. How were you a virgin in the first place, Sterling? You're not a nun, virgin birth aside."

She had to clear her throat, because she couldn't get up and run. He would catch her in an instant and she'd end up answering anyway, just with a greater display of his superior strength to be awed by when she did. She had absolutely no doubt.

"Well," she said after what felt to her like a very long while, though he didn't seem to move a muscle throughout it, "it wasn't a plan. It just happened."

"How does such a thing *just happen*?" His gaze moved over her, and some heretofore unknown romantic part of her thrilled to that expression on his harshly beautiful face then, as if it really was tenderness. And oh, how she wanted it to be. "You were a beautiful girl on her own when you went to New York. A cautionary tale, really."

She opened her mouth to tell him another lie, but she couldn't, somehow. It was as if everything really had changed, whether she liked it or not. It wasn't only the sex. It was the baby. The way he'd saved her from herself when she'd been out of her mind on hormones and guilt. It was that he hadn't hit her—had seemed astonished she'd thought he would. It was his gentleness now. It was the way he'd taken over her body so completely and yet still left her wanting more.

Who was she kidding? It was *him*.

And Sterling didn't want to think about what that meant. She thought she knew—and that was truly insane. But she couldn't lie to him, either. And there were different levels of the truth.

"My foster parents were the nicest people," she told him, smiling slightly as if that might make these things easier to talk about. As if anything could. "That's what everybody always said, in case we weren't grateful enough. They were kind. Giving. They took in kids like me who'd been otherwise completely abandoned. They had their own kids. They were active and responsible members of the community. Everyone adored them." She couldn't look away from him, though she wanted to. "And why wouldn't they? My foster parents never left any marks. Sometimes they just hit us and other times they liked to play elaborate games, using us as targets. They practiced their aim with cigarettes, cans. Sometimes forks and knives. But there were never any bruises anyone could see." She saw that dark thing move in his gaze and smiled again, deeper and harsher. "They always told us we were welcome to tell on them, if we dared. That they'd enjoy ripping little nothings like us apart in public. Because no one would ever believe a word we said about the saints of the neighborhood, and they were right."

"Where are these people now?" Rihad asked softly. Dangerously, as if, were he to speak in his usual voice, he would raze whole cities to the ground with the force of his fury.

And it made something long frozen deep within her unfurl in a little blast of warmth.

"They're behind me, that's where they are." She smiled at him, a real smile that time, and when he slid his hand along her cheek, she leaned into it. "But after that I knew how evil people were, once they thought they had all the power. How vicious and cruel. So I made myself into an Ice Princess who didn't like to be touched and was always much too sober to have any fun anyway, so everyone left me alone. And then Omar came along, and I didn't have to worry about that stuff anymore, because everyone believed I was with him. And that's how I accidentally ended up a virgin."

Rihad didn't speak for a long time, and she would have given anything to know what he was thinking. What was happening behind that austere, ruthless face of his and that disconcertingly sensual mouth. She wanted to lick him until neither one of them could think anymore. She wanted to bury her face in the crook of his neck, as if he could keep her safe from all the things that swirled around her that she couldn't even identify. He would, she thought. He really would.

And God help her, the things she wanted then, that she was too afraid to name.

"But you let me take you." His gaze was even more golden than usual then, and it set her alight. "Twice."

"Yes." Her throat was so dry that it hurt when she swallowed. "I did."

"Why?" He traced a line from the tender place beneath her ear, down and around to stroke the line of her collarbone, as if he was trying to smooth the ridge of it back beneath her skin. "Why me?"

"We're already married, Rihad," she said, as primly as if she was lunching at some terribly dignified country club. "Your name is on my daughter's birth certificate."

And she saw that smile of his again, watched it light up his eyes. It filled her with the same light.

"Why, Sterling. That makes you sound traditional and old-fashioned, not modern and scandalous at all."

"It seemed safe enough," she told him, caught in that glittering gaze of his. Lost in the way he was touching her, so casually intimate, as if this was only the beginning. As if there was so much further yet to go—but she didn't dare let herself think that. "And also, to be honest, I didn't think you'd notice."

He didn't seem to move, but everything changed. Got way more intense, so fast it made her stomach drop. "I noticed."

She froze. "Oh. Was I…? Was I not…?"

Rihad laughed then and rolled, coming up over her and holding her there beneath him, that stunning body of his stretched out above her, so gorgeously male it hurt.

"You were exquisite," he told her quietly, sincerity in every syllable. "You are a marvel. But I am old-fashioned myself, Sterling, as you've pointed out to me many times. Deeply traditional in every possible way."

She was shaking, and it wasn't fear. It was him. "I don't know what that means."

"It means that you were far safer when I thought you were a whore," he said bluntly, his dark gaze seeming to burn through her, kicking up new flames and changing everything. Changing *her*. "Now I know that you are only mine. Only and ever mine. And I, my little one, am a very, very selfish man."

And then he set about proving it.

CHAPTER ELEVEN

THE HEADLINE A MONTH LATER was like a slap—the hit,
perhaps, that Sterling had been expecting all along. She
sat frozen solid on the balcony outside Rihad's suite,
staring down at the tablet computer Rihad had left sitting there when he'd stepped inside to take a phone
call. She felt sick.

Black Widow Sterling Lures King Rihad into Her
Web! the worst of the European tabloids shrieked. And
the article beneath it was even worse.

> Sex-symbol Sterling flaunts postbaby bod and en-
> slaves the desert king! Starry-eyed King Rihad
> can't keep his eyes—or his hands!—off his late
> brother's lover. "But Sterling left a trail of broken
> hearts behind her in New York," say concerned
> friends. Will the formidable king be one more of
> heartbreaker Sterling's conquests?

It was beautifully done, really. Killer Whore. Vain
Whore. Married Whore. Omar's Whore. New York
Whore. So many clever ways of calling Sterling a whore
without ever actually uttering the word.

The worst part was, she hadn't seen this coming.

She hadn't expected it, and she should have. Of course she should have. But she'd actually believed that now that she and Rihad were not only married, but also actually as intimate as that honeymoon had been meant to suggest, the awful paparazzi would leave her alone.

She'd been incredibly naive.

There are no happy endings, she reminded herself then, frowning out at the sea that stretched toward the horizon before her as if basking, blue and gleaming, in the sun. *Not for you. Not ever.*

But she'd been lulled into believing otherwise.

Their lazy days at the oasis had bled together into one great burst of brilliant heat, a haze of bright sun above, desert breezes over the cool water in the shaded pools and the desperate, delirious *hunger* that only Rihad had ever called out in her—and that only he could satisfy.

Sterling had learned every inch of his proud, infinitely masculine body. She'd tasted him, teased him, taken him. She'd learned how to make him groan out his pleasure, how to scream out her own. He'd taken her beneath the endless stars, in the vast softness of his bed, in the luxurious tub that stood in her own luxuriously appointed tent. He'd been inventive and uninhibited— and demanding, as he'd promised. She'd learned to be the same in return.

Sterling had given herself over to the exquisite pleasures of the flesh that she'd denied herself so long— all her life, in fact. Touch. Lust. Desire and its sweet oblivion. She'd eaten too much, drunk too deeply. She'd lost herself in Rihad, again and again and again. She'd told him the truth about herself, or a critical portion of the truth anyway—and the world hadn't ended.

She'd let herself imagine that Rihad was as powerful

as he'd always appeared to her. That he could truly hold back whatever nightmares threatened. That he would.

That she and Leyla and this marvel of a man could create their own truths and live in them. That they could finally be the family she'd always wanted.

But she'd forgotten who she was.

She always did.

It had been some weeks since they'd left the oasis and it didn't take a genius to figure out why the tabloids had latched on to her again. The article went on to make salacious suggestions about a list of regional leaders and some local celebrities, all of whom had been at last night's elegant function in one of the new luxury hotel complexes being built along the shore of the Bay of Bakri.

That meant that someone at that party had taken exception to the Queen Whore being paraded about on their king's arm and had taken to the tabloids to express their feelings.

"I'd prefer you not read that nonsense," Rihad said from the doorway, his deep voice like a flame within her, that easily. That quickly. Sterling looked over at him, still frowning, despite the little flip her heart performed at the sight of him, dark and beautiful there in the arched entryway. His mouth crooked as if he could feel it, too. "It will rot your brain."

"I told you not to take me to your events, Rihad." When his fierce brows rose, she flushed, aware that her agitation had sharpened her tone. "I knew this would happen."

"It is our job to ignore the tabloids," he said, mildly enough. "Or so you told me yourself."

But this was different. *She* was a different person

than the woman who had said that to him. And *this* incarnation of herself didn't want to let the tarnish of *that* one seep into what they'd built between them in the past month. She thought it might break her apart.

"It's only going to get worse." Sterling folded her hands in her lap and tried to remain calm, or at least to look it. "It always gets worse. They already call me the Queen Whore."

"Not out loud or in print, they don't." There was no softness on his starkly beautiful face then. No hint of a curve to his lush mouth. Only that dangerous light in his dark gold eyes. "Not unless they wish to explain themselves to me personally. Let me assure you, no one does."

"You can't threaten everyone on the planet, Rihad. You can't *decree* that people forget my past."

"Your imagined past."

"What does that matter? When it comes to perception, all that matters is what people believe." She shook her head at him. "Isn't that why we went on our honeymoon in the first place?"

"It was one among many reasons," he said, and his dark gold eyes moved over her the way his hands did so freely, these days. And she was still so astonished that she liked it. That she more than *liked* it. "The least important, I think."

He looked dark and forbidding in the gleaming robes he'd worn today for his meetings with some of the local tribes later on, but he didn't intimidate her any longer. Not the way he once had. Now all that power, all that dark authority he wore so easily, made her shiver for entirely different reasons. His dark gold eyes fixed on hers and everything inside her stilled in glorious anticipation, the way it always did now. Goose bumps moved sinuously over her arms and shoulders, and she wished she could continue to lose herself in it. In him.

But she knew what he didn't.

That her past was a living thing that stalked her. It always would. It always did, because it lived inside of her. No matter what she did, or how, the world thought the worst of her. That wouldn't change. It had never changed. She'd told herself she was immune to it for all those years with Omar, because that kind of notoriety had been exactly what he'd wanted and they'd courted it together.

But Rihad was different. Rihad wasn't hiding. The last thing Rihad needed was notoriety.

Rihad deserved a whole lot better than a secondhand queen he'd married only for the baby's sake, no matter how they fit together in bed. Sex might have been new to Sterling, but it wasn't to him. He could get it anywhere, she reminded herself brusquely and ignored the deep pang inside her at the thought. He was the King of Bakri. There would be women lining the streets of Bakri City should he indicate he was looking.

Sterling was the one who couldn't imagine anyone but him touching her. She was the broken one, all the way through.

"You married yourself off to stop a scandal," she reminded him lightly, though nothing inside of her felt anything like light. It was as if the moment she'd acknowledged the darkness, it had seeped into everything. Every part of her. "Not to perpetuate one every time you step outside the palace walls."

He considered her for a moment, his dark gaze unreadable. He was still standing there in the arched doorway that led into his rooms, where she'd spent the bulk of her time since they'd returned from the desert. They hadn't even discussed it—he'd simply moved her things into his suite. Sterling had been so spellbound by this man it hadn't occurred to her to maintain any distance.

For his sake, not hers.

And it was then, frowning up at him, angry at herself and worried about his future, that Sterling understood that she'd fallen in love with Rihad al Bakri.

It stunned her. It was a hit as brutal as that tabloid headline, swift and to her gut, with the force of a hard kick. She didn't know how she managed to keep from doubling over. How she managed to keep looking at him as if her entire life hadn't run aground right then and there, decisively and disastrously.

Love wasn't something Sterling could do. Ever.

How had she managed to fool herself all this time? A baby. A husband. *No one will ever love you, little girl,* they'd told her. *This is what you deserve. Deep down, you know it.*

She did know it. And she never should have let all of this get so complicated.

"What can possibly be going through your head?" Rihad asked quietly, jolting Sterling's attention back to him. "To put such a look on your face?"

"I was only thinking about how soon we should divorce," Sterling said, in a surprisingly even tone of voice. There were too many things rolling inside of her, making her feel unsteady on her own feet, as if she was a storm about to break. "That's obviously the easiest and best way to solve this problem. You remain the dutiful, heroic king who married me only to secure

Leyla's position and when they discuss the scandal that is me, it won't affect you at all."

He'd gone so still. His dark gold eyes burned.

"Do I appear affected now?" It was a dangerous question, asked in that lethal tone of voice.

"It will make me seem particularly heartless and horrible if I were to leave before Leyla is a year old," Sterling continued matter-of-factly, not answering him. "That might be best, then. I trust that once everything's died down, once you marry someone far more appropriate, we can work out a quiet way for me to stay in her life."

"Sterling." He waited until she met his hard gaze, and she could admit that it was difficult. That it cost her. "What the hell are you talking about?"

"Our divorce," she said, struggling to keep her voice light. To gaze back at him as if there was something more inside her than a great weight and a terrible sob breaking her ribs apart. "Leyla is now legitimate. A princess of Bakri, as you planned. There's no reason to drag this out if my presence here is causing you trouble. That's silly."

"Because it has worked out so terribly for you thus far?" he asked, a hard edge in his voice, like a lash, and she had to force herself not to react to it. Not to show him how it had landed and how it hurt. "My condolences, Sterling. When you came apart beneath my mouth in the shower this morning, *twice*, I had the strangest impression that you'd resigned yourself to the horrors of this marriage. Somehow."

She crossed her arms beneath her breasts and made herself glare at him as if she still hated him—as if she'd ever really hated him—her heart pounding at her as if she was running. She wished she was.

Then again, this was how it had started.

"That's sex," she said dismissively, and she felt something sharp-edged scrape inside her as she said it. As if she wanted to hurt him. As if she wanted to remind him that this had never been meant to happen between them. As if he was to blame for the fact she'd lost herself in sex and happy fantasies of happy lives she could never have. As if loving him was something he'd done to her. A punishment for daring to imagine she could love anyone without repercussions, when she'd been taught otherwise a very long time ago. "I've never had it before, as you know. It turns out, it's a lot of fun."

"Fun," he repeated softly, in a way that should have terrified her.

She told herself it didn't. Or that it didn't matter either way.

"And I appreciate you introducing me to this whole new world," she said, never shifting her gaze from his. "I do."

"Introducing you?" he echoed, and that time, a chill sneaked down her back. Her heart already ached. Her stomach twisted. But if she loved him, if she loved her daughter—and God help her, but she did, so much more than she'd known she was capable of loving anything— she had to fix this.

And there was only one way to do that.

Maybe she'd always known it would come to this. Maybe that was why she'd never touched a man in her life. Because no matter who he was, it would always end up right here. Face-to-face with the worst of her truths and no way to escape it.

There is no other man, a small voice inside intoned,

like words chiseled into stone. Deep into her heart. *Not for you.*

She knew that was true, too. It didn't change anything.

"But you're not the only man alive, Rihad, regardless of how you act," she told him then, before she could talk herself out of it. Before she could give in to all the things she wanted. "You were merely my first."

For a moment Rihad held himself so still he thought he might have turned to stone himself, into one of the pillars that held up this palace of his, smooth and hard and cold all the way through.

Which would have been safer for Sterling by far.

Because what shook in him, rolling and buckling, seismic and intense, was so vast he was surprised the whole cursed palace didn't crumble down around them where they stood. There was a clutching sensation in his chest, a pounding in his head and a murderous streak lighting him up like a bloody lantern.

"I am your first, yes," he said, in the voice of the civilized man that he'd always thought he was, before her—a king, for his sins, not this wild, fanged creature within that wanted only to howl. Then stake its claim. "And your last, Sterling. Let us make sure that part is clear."

"That's not up to you," she said, tilting her chin up as if she was expecting a wrestling match to break out.

Rihad could think of few things he'd like more than to put his hands on her, but he wouldn't do it just then. Not while he was still battling his temper, which was all the more unpredictable because he was so unused to it.

He'd never understood desire. Need. This kind of exquisite weakness. Now he was made of nothing else.

He tried to remain calm. Or at least sound calm. "I think you'll find it is."

"There's no need to get so emotional," she chided, and he was as astonished as that day back in New York when she'd started issuing orders. She stood, smoothing her hands down the front of the long dress she wore over her bare feet, a combination he found maddeningly erotic. Or was that another *emotion*? He seemed to be full of them where she was concerned. "I don't know why you're not seeing this clearly. The sooner we divorce, the easier it will be to rehabilitate your image."

"My image is fine."

Sterling inclined her head toward the table and his tablet and all those snide tabloid articles. "Evidently not."

She even smiled serenely in his direction as she walked past him into the suite, the long skirt of her dress flowing out and around as she moved, so lithe and pretty on her feet it was as if everything she did was a dance. Even the way she walked away from him.

And this was absurd. He knew that. He knew she was trying to needle him, though he couldn't have said why. He knew she wanted him as much as he did her—he hadn't imagined their morning in his shower, the way she'd cried out his name and ground herself against his mouth, and he'd seen that same hectic fever in her gaze now, too. It was always there. Always.

He hadn't imagined everything that had happened between them over the past month. This woman was his in every conceivable way. He had no intention of divorcing her, or even permitting her to sleep apart from him again. What did it matter if she admitted this or not?

Yet Rihad found it mattered quite a lot.

He stalked after her, catching her while she was still crossing his bedchamber and using her elbow and her momentum to spin her back around to face him.

"Don't you dare—" she began, but he was already touching her, and that was its own alchemy.

That fire that only burned hotter by the day exploded between them, the way it always did, wild and bright. He saw her pulse accelerate in her neck. He saw that white-hot heat make her eyes go glassy.

"You little fool," he bit out, but this wasn't temper, he understood. Not any longer. There was that bittersweet pang of jealousy at the thought of her with other men, but everything else was pure, sensual menace that he had every intention of taking out on her delectable body. Until she took his point to heart. "Do you think this happens every day?"

"I assume it must," she fired back at him, so busy fighting him she didn't seem to notice the way he was backing her across the room, to the nearest wall. "Or every popular song I've ever heard is a lie."

She let out a small, surprised noise when her back came up against the nearest brocaded wall, and then another when Rihad merely leaned closer and pressed his forehead to hers, holding her that simply.

"This is the sex you seem to think you can get anywhere," he told her, and her mouth was a serious temptation, but he ignored it, concentrating on pulling that long skirt of hers up and sliding his hands beneath. "This is the chemistry you imagine is so run-of-the-mill."

He felt that shudder go through her and then his hands were on her soft thighs, and it was his turn to let out a long breath when he found she was completely bare beneath her dress. There was nothing but the heat of her skin, the touch of her soft curls, and then that molten core of her, all his.

Only and ever his.

"Rihad…" she whispered.

"I don't want to fight with you," he told her.

He angled his head back so he could look at her, even as he plunged a finger deep into her heat. He watched a flush spread over her cheeks and knew that was the truth of things between them. The only truth that mattered, and it always would be. That dark, bewitching fire. That endless well of need.

"If you have something to say to me, Sterling, say it. Don't poke at me. Don't pretend."

She stiffened at that. "Pretending is the problem. It's what we've—*I've*—been doing this whole time!"

"I don't think so."

He pulled his finger from her depths, then held her gaze as he licked it clean, her taste as intoxicating as ever on his tongue. He felt his mouth curve as her lips parted at that, as if she was finding it difficult to breathe regularly. He reached down between them to handle his robes and his trousers, and then he stepped between her legs as he lifted her up, wrapping her around him and holding her there for a long, hot instant.

This time, he didn't carry her to a nearby table. This time, as he lowered her against him he slid deep inside of her, so deep they both groaned at the sensation.

Her hands balled into fists at his shoulders and she bit her lip as if she meant to resist him. But then she rolled her hips against his as if she couldn't help herself, and Rihad smiled.

He took control then. Her ankles were locked tight around his hips and he lifted her up, then brought her down, working her against him slowly. So slowly. Making her shudder and pant. Making it so good she'd forget all this divorce and separation nonsense.

Because she was soft and hot, a revelation around him with every stroke, and she was his.

All his. Always his.

It took him a long while to realize that he was chanting that out loud, like a prayer or a promise, and when he did, he laughed.

"Say it," he demanded.

But this was Sterling, his Sterling. So even as she writhed against him, even as her hips met his in this wild dance of theirs, she defied him.

And God help him, he loved it. He loved all of this more than he'd ever imagined was possible, more than he'd ever loved anything or anyone. Sterling was his, damn it. All of her. Her body and her heart alike, and he didn't much care if she thought otherwise. He knew the truth.

He wasn't giving her up. Ever. Even if his kingdom came down around him. Even if the world followed suit.

For the first time in his life, he didn't care about his duty. He cared about her.

"Say it," he told her again. "I can do this all day. And if I can, you will. But you will not come until you admit what we both already know is the truth."

She let out a sound then, half fury and half need, and Rihad laughed again, because he was as hungry as she was. As greedy for her.

"All yours," she gritted out, her blue eyes slick and warm on his, and he felt it like a caress. This was who they were. Caress, capitulation, it was all the same thing. It all led to the same place. "Damn you, Rihad, I'm yours."

He reached down between them and pressed hard against the taut center of her hunger, and she bucked hard against him, arching her back and digging her fingers hard into his shoulders, then screamed as she plummeted over the edge.

But Rihad was only getting started.

CHAPTER TWELVE

STERLING HADN'T MEANT to eavesdrop.

She'd been enjoying the gala, held in the grand art gallery that was one of the jewels of the new Bakri City, a testament to the country's bright new future. Or so Rihad had said in his speech earlier, in English, for the benefit of the foreign press. She'd allowed the phalanx of docents to lead her through the first great exhibit, on loan from the Louvre, and had honestly enjoyed looking at the collection of world-class, world-famous art.

It had reminded her of her favorite way to spend a day in New York City: wandering aimlessly around the Metropolitan Museum of Art and losing herself in all the marvelous things collected there for the viewing, from paintings to metalwork to Egyptian tombs. Except here in Bakri City there was the sea on one side and the beckoning desert on the other, reminding her that she was across the world from the things she knew.

It had been ten days since she'd realized that she loved Rihad. Ten long days and longer nights since she'd understood that she must leave him and, worse, Leyla, too. Every day, she'd woken up and vowed that it would be her last in Bakri, that she would find a way to leave the two people she loved most. Yet somehow, there was always another reason to stay.

And here she was on yet another night, dressed in beautiful clothes as befit the queen she still had trouble believing was legitimately *her*. She'd smiled prettily on command, quite as if she couldn't see the speculation in every gaze that met hers. As if she couldn't hear the whispers that followed her around the great courtyard.

As if she wasn't aware that at least half of the people who spoke to her were thinking the word *whore* as they curtsied and called her *Your Majesty*.

"Your daughter is the bright jewel of the kingdom," professed one Bakrian aristocrat whom Sterling had recognized from her wedding. Where this woman and her husband, both possessed of crisp, upper-crust British accents when they spoke in their perfect English, had gazed back at her as if they couldn't understand a word she'd said.

"I certainly think so," Sterling had said.

"One can only hope she grows into her mother's beauty," said the husband, and Sterling hadn't much liked that look in his too-knowing eyes when he said it, or the way he'd leaned closer than was strictly appropriate when he'd continued. "What a blessing it is for a daughter to become like her mother in every way."

It took a moment for Sterling to understand that this person had, in effect, just called her infant daughter a whore. A *potential* whore.

She was going to ruin Rihad if she stayed. That much was obvious, no matter how he tried to dismiss it.

But aside from worrying over her biological limitations and the genetic propensity for ruining children she might have inherited from her own terrible mother,

Sterling hadn't really given a lot of thought to how her presence in Bakri would destroy *Leyla.* She'd thought that as Rihad's daughter in every way but her biology, Leyla would be safe. More than safe.

You should have known better, sneered that internal voice that she knew came from her foster parents, across all those years, as if she was still standing in the middle of that cold kitchen waiting for the next blow to lay her out on the linoleum floor. *You taint everything you touch.*

She'd ducked into one of the cordoned-off alcoves for a little breather after that unpleasant last encounter. She wanted to take a moment—only a moment—to let her face do whatever it wished. To drop her public smile. To simply not be on display.

Sterling pulled in a deep breath, then let it out. Then again.

And it was as she was preparing to walk back out and face it all again that she heard Rihad's deep voice from the other side of the pillar that concealed her.

"I have no worries whatsoever about the union between our countries," he was saying in his crisp, kingly manner. "Nor can I imagine that Kavian has indicated otherwise, to your publication or to anyone else."

That meant it was one of the reporters, Sterling understood, and that was why she didn't reveal her presence. She'd had enough of the press earlier, with their sugary smiles and all those jagged claws right underneath, sharpened on her own skin every time they asked her a pointed question.

"Yet your sister remains at large."

"The Princess Amaya's schedule remains private for obvious security reasons." Rihad's voice was so cold then it made Sterling's stomach clench tight. "But I can assure you that no member of the royal family is 'at large.' Your information is faulty."

"Neither Kavian nor Amaya have been seen—"

"His Royal Majesty Kavian ibn Zayed al Talaas, ruling sheikh of the desert stronghold Daar Talaas, is certainly not in hiding of any kind, if that is what your impertinent suggestion is meant to imply." Rihad's voice held dark warning then. "But he no more clears his schedule with me than I do with him. He certainly does not clear it with you. I would advise you to step away from this subject."

"Certainly, Sire." The man's voice made Sterling feel dirty. Tarnished. "My congratulations on your recent marriage."

Sterling winced then, at the thunderous silence that told her all she needed to know about the expression Rihad was likely wearing.

"Tread carefully," Rihad all but growled. "Very carefully."

"Certainly, Your Majesty, you must be aware that there is mounting concern among your subjects that a woman like that—"

"A woman like that?" Rihad's voice turned mild, which was her husband at his most volatile, even as that same old phrase knocked around inside of Sterling, leaving marks. New bruises to join the old. "By all means, enlighten me. A woman like what, exactly?"

That was when Sterling moved. She swept out from behind the pillar and hoped it would be assumed she'd simply taken herself off to the powder room.

Rihad stood squared off against a small, toad-like creature Sterling recognized as one of the paparazzi who had followed her every move in New York. She had no doubt that he was responsible for a great many of the horrible narratives that circulated about her to this day, as he'd taken after her as if Sterling was his pet project. He'd always looked at her as if he could *see* that truth buried deep inside of her. As if *he knew* how flawed and unwanted and *ruined* she truly was.

Part of her wanted nothing more than to leave him to Rihad's scant and rapidly eroding mercy, but she didn't dare. Not now, after all the recent bad press and a museum filled with more reporters. She was already enough of a stone draped around Rihad's neck, dragging him down. There was no need to add an assault-and-battery charge on her behalf to the list of her sins against this man.

"Sterling," the awful little man oozed at her. "We were just talking about you."

She didn't know which part of that offended her more—the way the man looked at her, the way he spoke to her with such unearned familiarity or the way he sidled closer to her with his hand extended as if he planned to put it on—

"Ancient Bakrian law states that if another man touches my queen without my permission I am not only permitted to rend him limb from limb with my own hands, but must do so to protect the honor of the crown," Rihad said conversationally, and the reporter froze. Rihad's smile didn't reach his eyes. "Barbaric, is it not? And yet so many of my subjects find comfort in the old ways."

He did not say, *myself included*, but Sterling felt certain she was not the only one who felt as if he'd shouted it from the rooftops.

The little man's eyes glittered with a sort of impotent fury that Sterling knew—she *knew*—would translate into yet another revolting piece about her in the morning papers. She could practically read the article now as it scrolled across the man's dirty mind.

To this man I will never be anything but a woman like that, Sterling thought miserably, but she only smiled at the reporter as she moved past him to take Rihad's arm. *The Queen Whore herself, parading around like so much pollution.*

"You shouldn't antagonize him," she said softly as Rihad drew her out onto the dance floor, the elegant crowd parting all around them to let them take its center, as if the tense exchange had never happened. "Not him or any of his little cronies."

"Must I introduce myself to you all over again?" Rihad's voice was arrogant, and his dark gold eyes still glittered furiously. "I am the King of Bakri. *He* should not antagonize *me*."

"You are the king, yes," she agreed, trying to keep her smile in place and her voice low, as befitted such genteel and public a place. "And you should not condescend to notice a man like him. That you do at all is my fault."

Sterling felt one of his hands tighten against the small of her back, and the other where his larger one gripped hers, and her curse was that she felt all of this like light. It was as if he poured straight into her, banishing all the darkness.

But she knew that wasn't true. She knew nothing could.

"Do not start this again," he warned her, his voice harsh despite his placid expression. "Not here."

"As you wish, Your Majesty," she murmured, so submissively that it startled a laugh out of him. Which in turn made her laugh, too, when she'd have said that was impossible under the circumstances. And still he spun her around and around that dance floor, as if they were nothing but beautiful. As if all of this was.

And some of the papers the next morning thought so, it was true.

But the others were vile.

There was a list of Sterling's supposed conquests, spanning the globe and including some countries she'd never visited and many men she'd never met. Another featured a list of her "raciest moments," which mostly involved skimpy outfits from her more outrageous modeling shoots held up as if she'd paraded around the streets of Manhattan wearing so little.

They didn't actually call her a whore. But then, they didn't have to call her anything. The comments section did that for them.

Sterling didn't mention the articles. Still, she could see the temper crack across Rihad's face and thought he tried to conceal it from her. Because that was Rihad, she understood now. Duty before all else. And he'd decided she was one of his duties. She cuddled Leyla on her lap and pressed kisses into the sweet crown of her head, and she only smiled when Rihad excused himself.

Because she knew what he refused to accept: this was never going to get better. *She* was never going to get better, or any less the subject of the repulsive speculation of the public.

And if she stayed here, Rihad and Leyla would rot right along with her.

Sterling might not have known a lot about love, but she knew—deep down she *knew*—that if she really, truly loved them, she wouldn't condemn them to that kind of life. Not when it took so little to save them.

So very little.

All she had to do was leave.

When his chief of security strode into Rihad's private conference room, scattering the gathered aides and the handful of ambassadors Rihad had been sitting with, he assumed it was about Amaya, at last.

"Has she been found?" he asked when the room was clear.

He thought the feeling that moved in him then was something far closer to regret than relief. But that made no sense. Amaya needed to be found and should have been found months ago. She needed to do her duty, no matter how Rihad might have come to sympathize with her plight. He hadn't lied to her when he'd told her there were no other options available to them.

But he couldn't deny the part of him that admired his younger sister for having stayed out of Kavian's reach all this time. Rihad liked the other man well enough. Respected him, even. But he doubted very much that any other creature on earth had led him on such a merry chase.

"We are tracking her, Your Majesty," his security chief said, standing at rigid attention, quite as if he expected a reprimand. "We have video of her leaving the palace an hour ago. It looks as if she's headed for the city limits."

Rihad digested that statement, and it took him longer than it should have to comprehend that the man was not talking about his sister.

But he couldn't make sense of what he was hearing.

He was aware that he'd frozen solid where he stood. He heard what his security chief was saying, but he couldn't seem to move. To react.

She had charmed her way into one of the palace's fleet of armored vehicles, because she was nothing if not persuasive when she wished. And because she was his queen. Instead of heading for the royal enclosure near the sea, a perfectly reasonable place for her to go without any guards because it was manned with its own, she'd had the driver change direction once they'd left the palace grounds and she'd headed for the far reaches of Bakri City.

There was nothing there, Rihad knew. Nothing save the border.

"My daughter," he managed to say, over the dark thud that was his heart in his chest. "Where is my daughter?"

His beautiful, perfect little Leyla, who he could not lose, and who, he realized, he'd never called *his* daughter before. Not out loud. He *would not* lose Leyla, no matter who her biological father was. She was his.

She and her treacherous mother were entirely his.

His security chief was muttering into his earpiece. Rihad was unnaturally still.

"The princess remains in the palace, Your Majesty. She is with her nurses even now."

"Excellent," Rihad bit out, and he started moving then, belting out orders as he went.

If Sterling had left the baby behind that meant he wouldn't have to temper his reaction when he found her—though he was sure he would have to think about that, at some point. That she'd taken off without her daughter, which was so unlike her as to be something like laughable.

He might have imagined, once, that Sterling was nothing more than a calculating, callous sort of creature. The kind of woman who would have a child for the sole purpose of tying herself to a man and, more to the point, his fortune.

That he didn't think that of her now, not even for a moment, told him things he was too furious to analyze just then. There was something seismic inside of him, bigger and bolder than anything he'd ever felt before. It was as massive as the desert, expanding in all directions, and he was not entirely certain he would be the same man when he survived it.

If he survived it.

But he had every intention of sharing the effects of it with his wife while he waited to see. Because he wasn't letting her go.

Not ever.

The helicopter landed with military precision on the dusty desert road, forcing Sterling's driver to slam on his brakes to a fishtailing stop—and putting an end to her escape fantasies that easily.

Sterling sat in the backseat and stared at the gleaming metal thing with its powerful rotors as if, were she to concentrate hard enough, she could make it go away again.

But it didn't. Of course it didn't.

For a long, shuddering moment, nothing happened. The helicopter sat there in the middle of the otherwise empty road. Sterling's driver, having lapsed into what sounded like frantic prayers as it had landed, was now muttering to himself. And that meant she had a lifetime or two to contemplate the leaping somersault her heart kept performing in her chest, no matter how sternly she told herself that *hope* was inappropriate.

She wasn't running away this time. She wasn't desperate or scared. She wasn't a fifteen-year-old kid and she was no longer afraid of her best friend's big, bad wolf.

This time, she was doing the right thing.

The helicopter's back door opened and Rihad climbed out, his movements precise and furious, and yet still infused with that lethal, masculine grace that made her mouth water. Maybe it always would.

But if so, it would happen from afar. In magazines or on the news.

She was no good for him. She was even worse for her precious daughter. Nothing else mattered

"Stay here," she told her driver, not that he'd offered to leap to her defense—the man clearly recognized the royal insignia on the helicopter's sides if not his king himself.

Sterling slammed her way out of the car into the hot desert sun. Memories assaulted her as the hot wind poured over her. Of facing Rihad much like this on a Manhattan street, in what seemed like a different lifetime. Of the dark look he'd worn then and the far darker and grimmer look he wore now.

Sterling didn't wait for him to reach her.

"What are you doing?" she threw at him across the hard-packed stretch of sandy road that separated them. "Let me go!"

"Never."

Short. Harsh. A kingly utterance and infused with all his trademark ruthlessness.

She was as instantly furious at him as she was pointlessly, traitorously moved by that.

"It wasn't a request."

"You do not give the King of Bakri orders, Sterling." He was closer then, and she could *feel* that edginess that came off him in waves, as if he was his own sun. "Your role is to obey."

"Stop this." Her voice was a hiss, and she slashed her hand through the air to emphasize it. "You're not being reasonable."

He was beyond furious—she could see it in every line of that body of his she knew better than her own now. He was practically vibrating with the force of his temper. And yet he only stared at her for a beat, then another, as if he couldn't believe she'd said that to him.

And then he tipped back his head and laughed.

He laughed and he laughed.

When he focused on her again, Sterling was shaking, and not from anything like fear. It was need. Longing. *Love.*

"I am renowned for my reason," he told her, no trace of laughter remaining in his voice then. "I am considered the most rational of men. My family is filled with emotional creatures who careened through their lives, neglecting their duties and catering to their weaknesses." He shrugged. "I thought I didn't have any weaknesses. But the truth is, I hadn't met you yet."

Again, she didn't know how to feel, so she ignored the great, swirling mess inside of her. She balled her hands into fists and scowled at him.

"You're making my point for me. I'm a weakness and you're a man who can't afford any. You need to let me go."

"Yet when it comes to you, Sterling, I am not the least bit reasonable," he growled at her. "Why the hell are you running away from me?"

"Why do you think?" she challenged, astonished. "I'm an anchor around your neck, weighing you down. You can't have this endless scandal and that's all this is. That's all I am."

"You left Leyla behind."

Sterling couldn't let herself think about that.

"She's better off," she gritted out. She swallowed back the anguished sob that threatened to pour out of her, to tear her open. "Divorced couples share custody all the time. There's no reason why we can't. And that means Leyla can grow up here, where she'll be safe."

"I can hear the words that come out of your mouth." His voice set every hair on her body on end. It prickled over her, harsh like sandpaper and a darkness beneath it. "Yet not one of them makes the slightest bit of sense."

"All I ask is that you find a good woman to help you raise her," Sterling pushed on, determined, despite the way everything inside of her lurched and rolled as if she was about to capsize herself. She couldn't let that happen. "Someone who is—"

"What?" Rihad asked brutally. "Not as dirty and ruined as you are?"

There it was.

It was shocking to hear someone else say that out loud after all these years. It was soul-destroying to hear it from him.

But Sterling wasn't running away from the only man

she'd ever loved like this, or ever would, because it was *easy*. She was doing it because it was *right*. Which meant she couldn't collapse at that. She couldn't let all that wild darkness inside of her take her down to her knees. It was too important that he accept this.

"You know, then." She couldn't process it.

He looked furious. Impatient. Darkly focused on her.

"I have an idea what those terrible people must have told you. It doesn't make it true."

"If you know," she managed to say, "then there's no reason for this to be so dramatic. I'm doing you a favor."

His expression shifted into something incredulous and arrogant at once.

"I do not want a favor, Sterling," he threw at her. "I want my family."

And that easily, he broke her heart.

"You can make yourself a perfect family," she told him, and she only realized as she spoke that her throat was constricted. That tears were welling up and pouring over, splashing down her face. It was as if he hadn't simply broken her heart—he'd broken *her* into a thousand tiny pieces and she couldn't keep them all together any longer. She wasn't sure she'd ever be able to do it again. "You can have more babies and a sweet, biddable wife who follows your commands and never shames you in public. You can—"

"*You* are my family!" he roared at her, and when she jumped back an inch he followed, taking her arms in those hard, surprisingly gentle hands of his. "You are my wife, my queen. We have a daughter. *This* is your family, Sterling. *I* am your family."

"Rihad—"

But her voice was choked and her words were lost

somewhere in a great, wild tangle that swamped her then. Far greater than fear. Far more encompassing.

"And I know that you love me, little one," he told her then, his voice lower, but still so raw it almost hurt to hear it. Almost. "Do you think I can't tell? When I do nothing but study you, day after day?"

"I don't," she managed to respond, though she couldn't stop shaking. "I can't. Nothing good ever comes of my loving something."

His hands tightened slightly on her arms, but his expression softened. He pulled her even closer. His dark gold eyes searched hers.

"Sterling." He said her name as if it was as beautiful as she'd thought it was when she'd picked it as a teenager. "I know that love for you means a hit must be forthcoming. I know you expect nothing but pain and misery when you dare to hope." He moved, rubbing his palms along her arms as if he was trying to warm her. Soothe her. *Love her.* "But I am a man of honor. My word is law. And no one will ever hit you again as long as you live. Especially not me."

She shook her head, hard, though shivers chased through her, one after the next as if she really was being torn apart. She could *feel* the tearing, deep inside of her.

"I'm your duty, nothing more," she said fiercely. "But your duty is to Bakri, not to me. And they deserve better. *You* deserve better."

"And you deserve to believe that you do, too."

She couldn't breathe past those words. She whispered his name again then, but she couldn't seem to stop crying. And then he let go of her, which was worse than a hit. Worse than a kick or two. She reached out a hand despite her intention to make him let her go, but then froze, because he wasn't walking away from her.

Rihad al Bakri, reigning sheikh, Grand Ruler and King of the Bakrian Empire, sank to his knees on the sand before her, never shifting that proud, stern gaze of his from hers.

He reached over, but he didn't take her hands. He took her hips in his powerful grip instead, as if he could lift her up if he wished. As if he could carry her forever, if she would only let him.

"I ordered you marry me once," he said in that low, dark, powerful voice of his. "Now I am asking you to stay with me. To live with me, love me, and who cares what the papers say. There are men watching us right now. Does it look as if that bothers me?"

"Rihad. You can't." But she didn't know what she meant to say and he wasn't listening to her anyway. His hands gripped her hips.

"I want to make more babies with you and this time, I want to hold them in my own hands as they enter this world. I want to make love to you forever. You are worth a thousand kingdoms, and mine is nothing but a pile of sand without you." His gaze was part of her, inside of her. "Be my wife in every possible way, Sterling. Not because it is my duty, but because it is my deepest wish. You are my heart. My love. I want you to be *mine*."

And she understood that vast, unconquerable thing that slammed down on her then. It wasn't fear—it was so much bigger. It was love. Real love, without conditions or qualifiers. Without lies. Love that might incorporate pain and darkness, as all life must in its time, but wasn't made of it.

She'd expected him to hurt her because that was all

she knew. She'd assumed she would ruin him the way she ruined everything, because that was what the people who'd hurt her had told her to justify their actions.

Terrible people, he'd called them.

But that was the past.

This man, here and now, on his knees before her in a way she imagined he'd never been before and never would be again, was the future.

She had to give herself over to the only thing she'd ever encountered that could beat back the darkness.

Love.

And within that, wrapped up so tightly it was nearly indistinguishable, *hope.*

"I'm already yours, Rihad," she whispered, fierce and hopeful at once. "I've been yours all along."

He wrapped his arms around her hips, resting his head against her stomach. She felt the press of his perfect mouth against her flesh and the deep shudder that went with it, as if she was accepting him into her bones.

"I love you," he told her, dark and imperious against the belly where she would bear his children. She knew she would, and not only because he'd decreed it. "Never doubt that."

"I love you, too," she said, her tears falling freely, but this time, they were made of joy. This time, she recognized it for what it was. This time, she believed it really would last forever. That they would, together. "I always will. And always is a very long time, I'm told."

"It had better be," he muttered, every inch of him the king.

And then she sank down beside him, and he took her in his arms, and for the first time in her life, Sterling let herself believe in forever.

CHAPTER THIRTEEN

Ten years later...

"He is very annoying, yes," Rihad told his furious daughter out in the private family garden that morning, and took care to hide his laughter from her. "But if you drown your brother in that pool, Leyla, there will be no party on Saturday and you may, in fact, spend your birthday in the dungeons."

"There aren't any dungeons in the palace," his ten-year-old replied, hotly. "Mama said you made that up."

He only smiled when she scowled at him. "There are dungeons if I say there are. I make the rules."

"Brothers are stupid," Leyla told him with a hint of imperiousness he thought she'd gotten directly from her mother.

Rihad thought of his own brother, lost so long now.

"I cannot forgive myself," he'd told Sterling on Omar's last birthday. As they did every year, they'd visited his grave on the palace grounds, together. "I doubt I ever will."

She had been wrapped in his arms, her back tucked against his front, his chin resting on her head.

"He'd already forgiven you," she'd said. She'd shifted

when he tensed. "He loved you, Rihad. He always loved you." She'd smiled up at him. "I was the one who hated you, for the both of us."

"Brothers might be stupid," he told Leyla now, "but you must love them anyway."

"Love sounds stupid, too," Leyla retorted, but she helped six-year-old Aarib continue to jump up and down on the wide lip of the pool near the waterfall anyway.

Though not without a very deep, long-suffering sort of sigh that did not bode well for her upcoming adolescence. Rihad repressed a shudder at that unhappy thought, given how stunning a child she already was, God help him. He returned his attention to the matters of state that awaited him on his tablet, a far more appealing prospect than his little girl growing up.

The papers hadn't always left them alone, but it was nothing as it had been. Rihad had seen to the dismissal of the particular reporters who dared hound his wife so relentlessly—just as he'd seen to the immediate exile of some of his courtiers when he'd finally seen the way they'd treated her.

The Queen of Bakri, by definition, was a woman without peer, spotless of reputation and widely beloved by all.

Ten years on, Rihad had the distinct pleasure of knowing that wasn't merely a decree he'd made, but the simple truth.

He knew the moment Sterling walked outside to join them in the garden. He always knew. She changed the air, he'd often told her, simply by breathing it, sharing it.

Those vicious, repulsive people she'd left behind in Iowa hadn't ruined her. She wasn't ruined. He thought that these days, she believed that without question at last.

His beautiful Sterling. His perfect wife.

He took a moment to marvel at her as she walked toward him across the stones while the world stilled all around him the way it always had. The way he thought it always would. She still dressed like the model she'd been, too elegant and so easily, offhandedly chic. That copper-blond hair of hers that still fascinated him beyond measure. Those long, long legs that had only this morning been draped over his shoulders as he'd driven them both to a hard, wild finish in the murky dark before dawn.

Ten years later and he was still hard at the thought of her.

"Are the monsters asleep?" he asked as she drew near.

"More or less." She smiled as she looked at Leyla and Aarib, as if she truly enjoyed the particular music of their young voices, scraping holes in the sky. He knew she did. Despite himself, so did he.

"God bless the morning nap."

Rihad thought of their younger boys, four-year-old Jamil and two-year-old Raza. Little hellions in every possible way, far louder than the older two combined, and they both demanded their mother's personal attention as only younger children could. "Indeed."

She moved as if to sit in her own seat but he pulled her down into his lap instead, nuzzling her neck until her breath caught. He pressed himself against the seam of her bottom, and she laughed.

"You're insatiable." But she sounded proud.

Content, he thought. They were content, and it was nothing like settling. It was like flying. Soaring through ten years and headed for ten more. Headed straight for forever.

"Only for you, my little one," he murmured against her ear. "Always for you."

They had not always had it easy, these past ten years. They had failed each other, hurt each other. The world was not always gentle and it was easy to lose each other in the whirl of children and responsibilities, even in a palace with fleets of nurses and around-the-clock staff.

But they had always had love. And love brought them back to each other, over and over again.

Rihad had learned to treat her less as a subject and more like a partner. Or he tried. She, in turn, had learned how to trust him.

This was intimacy, in all its complicated glory, of the soul and of the flesh. Lovers become parents, a king and his queen, a man and his woman. This was the magnificently double-edged sword of truly being known by another, across whole years.

In truth, he loved every bit of it.

And he still liked to show her how much.

"They're kissing." It was Aarib's disgusted little-boy voice, more piercing than usual, or perhaps Rihad wanted to be interrupted less in that moment.

"They do that a lot," replied Leyla, in her world-weary older-sister voice. "A *lot*."

"Why did we have more children?" Sterling asked him, laughing. "Whose terrible idea was that?"

But then she kissed him once more, and he saw moisture glistening in her lovely blue eyes. He ran his hand over her cheek.

"Thank you," she whispered. "Thank you so much, Rihad."

"For what?" he asked quietly.

"For everything," Sterling said, fiercely. "For giving me our family. For *being* my family."

She rose to go to the children then, and he let her leave, fully aware that she had no reason to thank him. She was the heart of this wondrous little tangle of theirs, love and trust and wonder, tears and scrapes and sudden furies.

Their heart. His heart.

His, Rihad thought. Forever.

And he was the king. His will was law.

* * * * *

MILLS & BOON®

The Thirty List

At thirty, Rachel has slid down every ladder she has ever climbed. Jobless, broke and ditched by her husband, she has to move in with grumpy Patrick and his four-year-old son.

Patrick is also getting divorced, so to cheer themselves up the two decide to draw up bucket lists. Soon they are learning to tango, abseiling, trying stand-up comedy and more. But, as she gets closer to Patrick, Rachel wonders if their relationship is too good to be true…

Order yours today at
www.millsandboon.co.uk/Thethirtylist

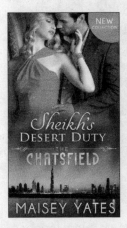

MILLS & BOON®

Why not subscribe?

Never miss a title and save money too!

Here's what's available to you if you join the exclusive **Mills & Boon Book Club** today:

- ✦ *Titles up to a month ahead of the shops*
- ✦ *Amazing discounts*
- ✦ *Free P&P*
- ✦ *Earn Bonus Book points that can be redeemed against other titles and gifts*
- ✦ *Choose from monthly or pre-paid plans*

Still want more?

Well, if you join today we'll even give you
50% OFF your first parcel!

So visit **www.millsandboon.co.uk/subs**
or call Customer Relations on 020 8288 2888
to be a part of this exclusive Book Club!

MILLS & BOON®

MODERN™

POWER, PASSION AND IRRESISTIBLE TEMPTATION

A sneak peek at next month's titles…

In stores from 19th June 2015:

- **The Ruthless Greek's Return** – Sharon Kendrick
- **Married for Amari's Heir** – Maisey Yates
- **Sicilian's Shock Proposal** – Carol Marinelli
- **The Sheikh's Wedding Contract** – Andie Brock

In stores from 3rd July 2015:

- **Bound by the Billionaire's Baby** – Cathy Williams
- **A Taste of Sin** – Maggie Cox
- **Vows Made in Secret** – Louise Fuller
- **One Night, Two Consequences** – Joss Wood

Available at WHSmith, Tesco, Asda, Eason, Amazon and Apple

Just can't wait?
Buy our books online a month before they hit the shops!
visit www.millsandboon.co.uk

These books are also available in eBook format!